Arthur Henry Bullen, Nicholas Breton

Poems, Chiefly Lyrical, from Romances and Prose-Tracts of the Elizabethan Age

With Chosen Poems of Nicholas Breton

Arthur Henry Bullen, Nicholas Breton

Poems, Chiefly Lyrical, from Romances and Prose-Tracts of the Elizabethan Age
With Chosen Poems of Nicholas Breton

ISBN/EAN: 9783337413644

Printed in Europe, USA, Canada, Australia, Japan

Cover: Foto ©Andreas Hilbeck / pixelio.de

More available books at **www.hansebooks.com**

POEMS,

CHIEFLY LYRICAL,

FROM ROMANCES AND PROSE-TRACTS OF
THE ELIZABETHAN AGE:

WITH CHOSEN POEMS OF NICHOLAS BRETON.

EDITED BY

A. H. BULLEN.

LONDON:
JOHN C. NIMMO,
14, KING WILLIAM STREET, STRAND.
1890.

INTRODUCTION.

IN the present volume I offer yet another collection of Elizabethan verse to the admirers of
our old poets. Davison's "Poetical Rhapsody"
will follow without delay: and then I have done.
Ne quid nimis.

When I excused the absence of Greene and
Lodge from my anthology, "Lyrics from Elizabethan Dramatists," I announced that I intended
to issue a collection of poems from Elizabethan
romances. I must confess that, on proceeding to sift
the poetry which is so copiously scattered through
the old prose romances, I was somewhat disap-
pointed. Much of it is of indifferent value and falls
far below the standard of excellence that I have tried
to preserve in my other anthologies. So I determined to alter my plan. Instead of devoting a
whole volume to the romances, I have divided the
anthology into three groups. The first contains

poems from the romances; in the second I have
assembled Nicholas Breton's choicest poems; and
the third embraces lyrics from Clement Robinson's
"Handful of Pleasant Delights," and from "The
Phœnix' Nest." Breton's poems are not readily accessible, and certainly deserve attention. Clement
Robinson's collection and "The Phœnix' Nest" are
—with the exception of "Tottell's Miscellany"—
the most interesting of the miscellanies issued
before 1600, the year of the publication of
"England's Helicon."

A learned and genial French scholar, M. Jules
Jusserand, gave us a year or two ago an excellent
account of the Elizabethan novel. He has recently
revised and enlarged his essay, which is presently
to make its appearance in English dress. As the
field is occupied by M. Jusserand, it is unneces-
sary for me to touch on the history of the early
novel. I am concerned only with the poetry of
the Elizabethan romances. The old Greek novelists
—Heliodorus, Longus, Achilles Tatius, and the
rest—did not garnish their stories with verse; and
Apuleius stuck to prose. It was from Italy and
Spain that our romance-writers caught the habit of
mingling verse with prose. Almost invariably they
were indebted for their plots to foreign originals;
and not seldom the verse with which they sought
to relieve the tedium of their narratives was "con-
veyed" from over-sea. Gervase Markham, in the

preface to his "English Arcadia," remarked that
Sir Philip Sidney lay under some obligation to a
Spanish romance, once highly esteemed in England, the "Diana" of Jorges de Montemayor,
(and he might have added that Sidney was also
indebted to Sannazarro's "Arcadia"). A translation
of "Diana" was made by Bartholomew Yong, or
Young, as early as 1584, but was not published until 1598. Yong did not succeed in rendering the
poetry neatly ; but the editor of "England's Helicon" devoted many pages of his anthology to
Yong's translations. As for the poetry in Sidney's
"Arcadia," it is undeniably disappointing. If we
want to see how true a poet Sidney really was, we
must go to the songs and sonnets of Astrophel and
Stella, not to the "Arcadia." In his romance he
indulges his fondness for metrical experiments ; he
sports in hexameters, asclepiads, sapphics, etc.—
feats of agility that quickly exhaust the reader's
patience.

Thomas Lodge candidly acknowledges at times
his indebtedness to foreign originals. In "A Margarite of America," 1589, he gives us renderings of
several Italian sonnets, and mentions the authors'
names. But he is not always careful to express his
obligations. In "Scylla's Metamorphosis," 1589,
he has the following dainty poem :—

> "The earth late choked with showers,
> Is now arrayed in green ;

Her bosom springs with flowers,
　The air dissolves her teen :
The heavens laugh at her glory,
Yet bide I sad and sorry.

The woods are decked with leaves,
　The trees are clothed gay ;
And Flora, crowned with sheaves,
　With oaken boughs doth play ;
Where I am clad in black,
The token of my wrack.

The birds upon the trees
　Do sing with pleasant voices,
And chant in their degrees
　Their loves and lucky choices ;
When I, whilst they are singing,
With sighs mine arms am wringing.

The thrushes seek the shade,
　And I my fatal grave ;
Their flight to heaven is made,
　My walk on earth I have ;
They free, I thrall ; they jolly,
I sad and pensive wholly.

These verses have been justly admired, but it has
not been noticed that they are closely imitated
from the opening stanzas of a longer poem of
Philippe Desportes :—

　　"La terre, naguère glacée,
　　Est ores de vert tapissée,
　　Son sein est embelli de fleurs,

L'air est encore amoureux d'elle,
Le ciel rit de la voir si belle,
Et moi j'en augmente mes pleurs.

Les bois sont couverts de feuillage,
De vert se pare le bocage,
Ses rameaux sont tous verdissants ;
Et moi, las ! privé de ma gloire,
Je m'habille de couleur noire,
Signe des ennuis que je sens.

Des oiseaux la troupe légère
Chantant d'une voix ramagère,
S'égaye aux bois à qui mieux mieux :
Et moi tout rempli de furie
Je sanglotte, soupire, et crie
Par les plus solitaires lieux.

Les oiseaux cherchent la verdure :
Moi je cherche une sépulture,
Pour voir mon malheur limité.
Vers le ciel ils ont leur volée :
Et mon âme trop désolée
N'aime rien que l'obscurité."

Desportes was widely read in England. Indeed, Lodge, in "A Margarite of America," speaks of his "poetical writings" as "being already for the most part Englished and ordinarily in every man's hands." This seems to be an exaggeration, but there can be no doubt that Desportes had some influence on English poetry. One of the finest poems in the present volume is the passionate address (from "The Phœnix' Nest") beginning :—

"O Night, O jealous Night, repugnant to my measures ![1]
  O Night so long desired, yet cross to my content !
There's none but only thou that can perform my pleasures,
  And none but only thou that hindereth my intent."

This first stanza is clearly out of Desportes :—

"O Nuit, jalouse Nuit, contre moi conjurée,
  Qui renflammes le ciel de nouvelle clairté,
T'ai-je donc aujourd'hui tant de fois désirée
  Pour être si contraire à ma félicité ? "

But the anonymous English poet confines his imitation to the first stanza. The later stanzas have nothing in common with the French poem ; and I do not hesitate to say that the English verses are far richer and more fervid than anything written by Desportes. The triumphant extravagance of the final stanza is hardly to be found outside of our Elizabethan poets :—

" And when my will is wrought, then, Cynthia, shine, good
    lady,
  All other nights and days in honour of that night,
That happy heavenly night, that night so dark and shady,
  Wherein my Love had eyes that lighted my delight ! "

It seems to me that whenever Lodge imitates Desportes, he greatly improves upon his model. Desportes has a sonnet beginning :—

---

[1] Old ed. "pleasures," which recurs in the third line. The repetition would be intolerable.

"On verra défaillir tous les astres aux cieux,
Les poissons à la mer, le sable à son rivage,
Au soleil ses rayons bannisseurs de l'ombrage,
La verdure et les fleurs au printemps gracieux :
Plutôt que la fureur des rapports envieux
Efface en mon visage un trait de votre image."

Compare this with Lodge's poem (p. 43) beginning :—

"First shall the heavens want starry light,
The seas be robbed of their waves ;
The day want sun, and sun want bright,
The night want shade, the dead men graves ;
    The April flowers and leaf and tree,
    Before I false my faith to thee."

Desportes' sonnet is a bundle of dry conceits ; Lodge's song is musical as a running brook.

Lodge's lyrical measures have frequently a flavour of Ronsard. He does not adopt the metres invented by Ronsard, but his own inventions seem to have been inspired by Ronsard's example. In a curious work entitled "Tarlton's News out of Purgatory," issued anonymously in 1590, we have (what I take to be) a sly parody on Lodge's Ronsardian poetry. The writer (possibly Thomas Nashe) introduces us to a company of poets assembled in Purgatory, and we are entertained with a love-poem that professes to be by Ronsard. As the passage is of some interest, I make no apology for quoting it entire (in the old spelling) :—

"The tale of the Painter being ended, passing a

little further, I might see where sat a crew of men that
wore Baye garlands on their heads, and they were
Poets; amongst which was olde Ennius, Virgill,
Iuuenall, Propertius, and wanton Ovid, Martial,
Horace, and many moe which had written las-
civious verse or other heroicall poems.   But above
them all I markęd olde Ronsard, and he sat there
with a scroule in his hand, wherein was written the
description of Cassandra his mistresse, and because
his stile is not common, nor haue I heard our
English Poets write in that vaine, marke it, and I
will rehearse it, for I haue learned it by hart.

RONSARD'S DESCRIPTION OF HIS MISTRIS, WHICH HE WERES IN HIS HANDS IN PURGATORY.

Downe I sat,
I sat downe,
   Where *Flora* had bestowed her graces:
Greene it was,
It was greene
   Far passing other places:
      For art and nature did combine
      With sights to witch the gasers eyne.

There I sat,
I sat there,
   Viewing of this pride of places:
Straight I saw,
I saw straight,
   The sweetest fair of all faces:
      Such a face as did containe
      Heavens shine in every veine.

I did looke,
Looke did I,
  And there I saw Apollos wyers : ·
Bright they were,
They were bright ;
  With them Auroras head he tires.
    But this I wondred how that now
    They shadowed in Cassanders b[r]ow.

Still I gazde,
I gazde still,
  Spying Lunas mylke white glasse :
Commixt fine,
Fine commixt,
  With the mornings ruddie blase :
    This white and red their seating seeks
    Upon Cassandraes smiling cheekes.

Two stars then,
Then two stars,
  Passing Sunne or Moone in shine,
Appearde there,
There appearde,
  And were forsooth my mistris eine,
    From whence prowd Cupid threw his fire
    To set a flame all mens desire.

Brests she had,
She had breasts,
  White like the silver dove ;
Lie there did,
There did lye,
  Cupid ouergrowne with love :
    And in the vale that parts the plaine
    Pitcht his tent there to remaine.

This was she,
She was this,
  The fairest fair that e'er I see,
I did muse,
Muse did I,
  How such a creature fo[u]nd could be :
    A voice replied from the Aire,
    Shee alone and none so faire."

There can be no doubt that this poem is a clever parody, not to be taken seriously. "Tarlton's News" was licensed for publication in June, 1590 ; and Lodge's "Rosalynd" was licensed later in the same year. But, after the fashion of the time, "Rosalynd" had doubtless been circulated in MS. before publication. If we turn to "Rosalynd," I think that we shall have no difficulty in discovering the poem at which the parodist was poking his fun. It was surely "Montanus' Sonnet," beginning :—

  " Phœbe sat,
Sweet she sat,
  Sweet sat Phœbe when I saw her. . . .

Phœbe sat,
By a fount,
  Sitting by a fount I spied her," etc. (pp. 44-5.)

The repetition

  " Phœbe sat,
Sweet she sat,"

is risky ; but

> " Down I sat,
> I sat down,"

is intentionally absurd. Lodge's poem is not written in one of Ronsard's metres, but it certainly has something of the Ronsardian spirit. At least the jocular author of "Tarlton's News" discovered a resemblance between Ronsard and Lodge. It would be interesting to discuss what debt our old lyrists really owed to Ronsard and his circle ; and I hope to take up the enquiry hereafter.

Robert Greene's romances and love-pamphlets are insipid reading ; but the poetry interspersed is frequently excellent. There is no sweeter cradle-song than "Weep not, my wanton, smile upon my knee" (p. 15), which was written about the time when he cruelly deserted his wife and young child. The story of his miserable life is too well known. He died at thirty, worn out by his excesses. In his last sickness none of his boon companions came near him ; but he was visited by a former mistress, the mother of his son Fortunatus. He lay in the squalid house of a poor shoemaker near Dowgate : and on the day before his death he wrote that most pathetic letter to the wife whom he had abandoned,—" Doll, I charge thee, by the love of our youth and by my soul's rest, that thou

b

wilt see this man paid; for if he and his wife had not succoured me, I had died in the streets. Robert Greene." His pious hostess, in obedience to his last injunction, crowned his dead body with a garland of bays. Though his life was irregular, no charge of depravity can be brought against his writings. Throughout his novels he was careful to inculcate rules of virtuous conduct. He lived in the baser parts of London, consorting with thieves and sharpers; but he sang of " Flora and the country-green," of wise content and quiet simplicity.

From " The Mirror of Knighthood," a translation of the famous Spanish romance " Espeio de Principes y Cavalleros " (which the curate in " Don Quixote " condemned to the flames) I have gathered some poems that will doubtless be new to the reader. The English translation is in nine volumes, which were published at various dates ranging from 1583 to 1601. Only one perfect copy, preserved among Douce's books in the Bodleian library, has come down ; and it would be safe to say that no living person has read through the nine volumes. But in Elizabeth's days the book was highly esteemed, particularly by romantic prentices and waiting-maids. Sir Thomas Overbury, in his character of " A Chamber-Maid," tells us—" She reads Greene's works over and over, but is so carried away with the " Mirror of Knighthood," she is many times resolved to run out of herself and become a lady-errant." The first part was turned into English by a lady, Margaret Tyler, who begged the critics to deal gently with her translation on the ground that "it is a womans woorke, though in a story prophane and a matter more manlike than becommeth my sexe." Her apology for undertaking the work is engaging and ingenious. She sees men dedicating books tò ladies; and she urges that, if ladies are allowed to read the books so dedicated, they should have liberty to "farther wade," for "it is all one for a woman to pen a storie as for a man to addresse his storie to a woman." Some ill-natured people might suggest that, if she wanted to try her hand at translation, she should have chosen a book of divinity. But in matters of controversial divinity she dared not trust her own judgment; and such Spanish books of divinity as she had read would be sure to "breed offence to some." She foresees that some churlish persons, who are able to read the original, will object to see "theyr Spanish delight tourned to an English pastime;" but she contents herself with remarking "What nature such men be of I list not greatly dispute." Margaret Tyler went no further than Part I.; Parts II.-IV. were translated by "R. P." (Robert Parry?); Parts· V.-VI. appeared anonymously; and a certain "L. A." was responsible for Parts VII.-IX.

An indefatigable translator and adapter was Anthony Munday. In the preface to my edition of "England's Helicon" I spoke slightingly of Munday; I pointed out how poor is the quality of the poetry in his "Banquet of Dainty Conceits," and scouted the notion that he should be identified with the "Shepherd Tony." But Munday rose in my estimation when I found in his pageant "Metropolis Coronata" the blithe song of Robin Hood and his Huntsmen (printed in "Lyrics from Elizabethan Dramatists," p. 87),—a song which immediately established his claim to the dirge in "The Death of Robert Earl of Huntingdon" (*ibid.* p. 86). It became clear to me that on rare occasions this tedious old writer (who has been irreverently styled "The Grub Street patriarch") must have been genuinely inspired; and I began to suspect that, after all, he might be the Shepherd Tony of "England's Helicon." In his very rare book "Zelanto, the Fountain of Fame," 1580, I found a tunable love-ditty. But my surprise was great when, in turning over his "Primaleon," 1619, I came upon the most famous of the Shepherd Tony's poems "Beauty sat bathing by a spring;" and I am now driven to conclude that Anthony Munday is the Shepherd Tony. "Primaleon" was originally written in Castilian; but Munday's translation is stated on the title-page to have been made "out of French and Italian." So far as I have observed, he has kept closely to the French version (of Gabriel Chappuis) ; but the poetry is his own addition, and is not found in the French copy.

Among the other romance-writers from whom I have quoted are John Dickenson (whose fluent quatrains on "Cupid's Journey to Hell" take the ear pleasantly) and Lady Mary Wroth, Sir Philip Sidney's niece, authoress of "Urania." Ben Jonson dedicated his "Alchemist" to Lady Mary Wroth, and in "Underwoods" published a handsome sonnet in praise of her poetry. She was a woman of brilliant parts, who had the misfortune to be married to a jealous husband. Jonson's chivalrous compliments were perhaps more appreciated by the lady than by her husband Sir Robert :—

> " in your verse all Cupid's armory,
> His flames, his shafts, his quiver, and his bow,
> His very eyes are yours to overthrow."

Scanning the poetry with a critical eye, I could not find much that was satisfactory.

Nicholas Breton, from whom I have quoted largely, began to write as early as 1575, and continued to issue books and pamphlets, in verse and prose, down to 1626, in which year he is supposed to have died. He was a very versatile writer, and has given us moral and religious poems, satires, romances, books of character, a complete letter-writer, pastorals, and what not ?

The most attractive of all his books, to my thinking, is "The Passionate Shepherd," 1604, a small collection of "pastoral verses written by the Shepherd Bonerto [*i. e.* Breton] to his beloved Shepherdess Aglaia." It is one of the very best specimens of a style of poetry that was much cultivated in Elizabethan times. Breton wrote always in great haste, and never indulged in the luxury of revision. He frequently allows his rhymes to carry him along, and lets the sense shift for itself. We may not be quite sure at times in reading "The Passionate Shepherd" that the grammatical constructions are nicely adjusted, and fastidious critics may complain that the writing is too diffuse. But the poet is in his gayest humour; we are charmed by the easy flow of his verse, and should be churls if we were not warmed by his enthusiasm. The pastoral beginning "Who can live in heart so glad?" (p. 108) is sustained throughout with the liveliest spirit, and ends with a gallant flourish :—

> " Had I got a kingly grace,
> I would leave my kingly place
> And in heart be truly glad
> To become a country lad ;
> Hard to lie, and go full bare,
> And to feed on hungry fare ;
> So I might but live to be
> Where I might but sit to see

Once a day, or all day long,
The sweet subject of my song :
In Aglaia's only eyes
All my worldly paradise."

There is always something of artificiality about pastoral poetry; but Breton loved the country and kept an observant eye. Quaintly and pleasantly he tells of the subtle fox—

" How the villain plies the box :
After feeding on his prey,
How he closely sneaks away
Through the hedge and down the furrow
Till he gets into his burrow " ;

and with what friendly interest he watches

" the black-haired coney
On a bank or sunny place
With her forefeet wash her face " !

Breton was very popular, and in consequence unscrupulous publishers sometimes made free with his name. In 1591 was published a book called " Brytons Bowre of Delights," of which a unique copy is preserved in a private library. I have not been able to see this book, but in "The Pilgrimage to Paradise " Breton distinctly states that he wrote only a few of the poems. Another collection of similar character is " The Arbour of Amorous Devices . . . " by N. B., Gent., 1593-4, of which a unique copy, unfortunately imperfect, is preserved among the books that Edward Capell bequeathed to Trinity College, Cambridge. Here is found the beautiful cradle-song, "Come, little babe, come, silly soul," (p. 92).[1]

Though I have some liking for Breton's devotional poems, I can hardly allow that they are of the first quality. He has been ranked with Southwell and Crashaw; but this estimate is too high. The poet to whom he bears nearest resemblance in his religious musings is John Davies of Hereford. Both Davies and Breton could spin off any quantity of devotional verse (respectable verse too), when the feeling seized them; but their fluency is very tiresome. Still the reader will find something to admire in the excerpts that I have given from Breton's religious poetry. Let him turn to the stanzas beginning, "Men talk of love that know not what it is" (p. 105).

More interesting than the religious poetry is the collection of lyrical poems "Melancholic Humours in verses of divers natures," 1600, to which Ben

---

[1] In the Percy Folio MS. we have a cradle-song, "Balow, my babe, ly still and sleepe," of which several versions (more or less corrupt) were published in broadside form. It has been ignorantly claimed as a Scotch song ("Lady Anne Bothwell's Lament"). Rev. J. W. Ebsworth, in his "Roxburghe Ballads," Vol. VI., pt. xviii, pp. 575-580, points out that all the "Balow" lullabies are poor imitations of "Come, little babe." He is rightly contemptuous on the subject of "the supposed Scottish origin, a hundred years too late, and all the senseless chatter about Lady Anne Bothwell."

Jonson prefixed a commendatory sonnet.   Breton
is fond of playing on words and phrases, bandying
them to and fro, saying the same thing in a dozen
different ways, chasing a conceit about and about.
It is not very exalted work, but the rhymes have a
pleasant tinkle.   One of the most characteristic
examples of this playful style is "Farewell, love,
and loving folly" (p. 97).   If he had lived in these
days, he would have no doubt helped to revive the
old French forms, and would have given us rondels,
virelayes, triolets and the like.   In "England's
Helicon" we have some of the best of his lyrical
poems.[1]   Dr. Grosart in his edition of Breton's
works printed, from a MS. in private hands, some
poems that had not previously found their way into
print.   Though it would not be right for me to
poach on his preserves, there can be no harm in
quoting here one little poem, a description of love-
making in the happy days of pastoral simplicity,
when girls did not look for costly presents (rings,
chains, etc.) from their lovers, but were content
with a row of pins or an empty purse,—the days
when truth was on every shepherd's tongue and
maids had not learned to dissemble.   Whether
there ever was such a time, since our first parents

---

[1] In the present volume I have not included any poems of
Breton that are found in "England's Helicon," for I suppose
that the majority of readers will have my edition of that
anthology.

were driven out of Paradise, we need not stop to
enquire. The old poets loved to talk about it;
and this is what Breton has to say :—

> " In time of yore when shepherds dwelt
>   Upon the mountain-rocks ;
> And simple people never felt
>   The pain of lovers' mocks :
> But little birds would carry tales
>   'Twixt Susan and her sweeting,
> And all the dainty nightingales
>   Did sing at lovers' meeting :
> Then might you see what looks did pass
>   Where shepherds did assemble,
> And where the life of true love was
>   When hearts could not dissemble.
>
> Then *yea* and *nay* was thought an oath
>   That was not to be doubted,
> And when it came to *faith* and *troth*
>   We were not to be flouted.
> Then did they talk of curds and cream,
>   Of butter, cheese, and milk ;
> There was no speech of sunny beam (?),
>   Nor of the golden silk.
> Then for a gift a row of pins,
>   A purse, a pair of knives,
> Was all the way that love begins ;
>   And so the shepherd wives.
> But now we have so much ado,
>   And are so sore aggrieved,
> That when we go about to woo
>   We cannot be believed ;
> Such choice of jewels, rings, and chains,
>   That may but favour move,

> And such intolerable pains
>   Ere one can hit on love ;
> That if I still shall bide this life
>   'Twixt love and deadly hate,
> I will go learn the country life
>   Or leave the lover's state."

As a satirist Breton had little of the "saeva in-dignatio," real or assumed, of Marston or Hall; and from his satirical or semi-satirical writings, we really gain a truer insight into the manners of the time than can be got from more violent writers. There was nothing ill-natured or acrimonious about Breton ; he might have said with Ben Jonson (but with less fear of contradiction)—

> " All gall and copperas from his ink he draineth ;
> Only a little salt remaineth."

His satirical reflections will sometimes strike a modern reader as curiously apt.   In his denuncia-tion of the rich upstart (a standing dish for satirists) he is neat and happy :—

> " He shall have ballads written in his praise,
> Books dedicated to his patronage,
> Wits working for his pleasure many ways,
> Pedigrees sought to mend his parentage,
> And linked perhaps in noble marriage."

As a character-drawer he was not so terse and epigrammatic as Overbury, but he was far more genial.   "The Good and the Bad," 1616, is much in the manner of Fuller's "Holy and Profane State." Indeed Fuller seems to have closely studied these characters of Breton; but he has improved upon them, for he had—it is needless to say—a richer vein of humour, a sounder and profounder knowledge of the world, a pithier expression.

One of his most entertaining books is his "Fantastics," a series of brief prose essays on "The World," "Love," "Money," "Spring," "Summer," "Harvest," "Winter," etc. He has a word to say about each of the twelve months; and then he sketches Christmas Day, Lent, Good Friday, and Easter Day. One's spirits droop at the description of Lent; but with what gusto he dwells on the joyousness that succeeds that season of sorrow,— when on Easter Day the starveling Jack-o'-Lent is turned out of doors; when the fishermen hang up their nets, and the calf and the lamb walk toward the pantry; when the air is wholesome and the sky comfortable! Another entertaining book, which was very popular throughout the seventeenth century, is "A Post with a Packet of Mad Letters,"[1] first printed in 1603 and afterwards enlarged, a manual of correspondence for persons of all ages and every degree.

Breton's novel "The Miseries of Mavillia, the

---

[1] I have quoted some of these letters in the Notes at the end of the volume.

most unfortunate lady that ever lived," 1599, is dismissed with contempt by Dunlop (who had probably never read it) in his " History of Fiction," but I found it interesting.[1] Some of Breton's tracts are, it must be owned, of the thinnest texture, written merely to introduce a good anecdote; as in the case of " Grimello's Fortunes," 1604, where we have the pretty jest of the Eel and the Magpie.[2] Not the least whimsical of his writings is his " Crossing of Proverbs," 1616, where he first gives a proverb and then proceeds to take exception to it, as thus :—" Two may keep counsel if the third be away.—Not if a woman be one "; " A bird in the hand is worth two in the bush.—Not if they be fast limed;" " 'Tis merry when gossips meet.—Not if they fall out about the reckoning."

It is only in his moral and didactic writings that Breton is ever tedious. His prose, which is always quaint and neatly turned, is valuable for the bright, cheerful pictures that it gives of Elizabethan society; and his lyrical poetry at its best is very good indeed.

Clement Robinson's miscellany " A Handful of Pleasant Delights " was licensed for publication in the summer of 1561 under the title of " A boke of very pleasaunte Sonettes and storyes in myter"; but

---

[1] In the Notes I give an account of " Mavillia."
[2] See the Notes for the tale of the Eel and the Magpie.

the earliest extant edition, preserved in an imperfect unique copy, is dated 1584. Some of the poems in the 1584 edition were certainly written after 1561. Robinson edited the volume, but it is not known whether he wrote any of the poetry. The name "Peter Picks" (a fictitious personage, I suppose) is subscribed to some poems; and others profess to be by "I. Tomson," whoever he may have been. All the poems were intended to be sung to one or other popular tune. For instance, "Maid, will ye love me, yea or no?" was to be sung to the tune of "The Merchant's Daughter went over the Field" (a tune with which I am not acquainted). Sometimes we are left to choose our own tune. Thus, "I smile to see how you devise" might be sung "to any pleasant tune." I have included four songs from the miscellany,—light, careless ditties.

From "The Phœnix' Nest," edited in 1593 by a certain "R. S.," I have chosen some of Lodge's best lyrics and some good anonymous verse. At one time I had thought of printing the "Phœnix' Nest" in full; but it is not altogether a satisfactory anthology, and some of the choicest poems are accessible in "England's Helicon" and in other collections. It will be found that there is not much spicery left in the Nest when we have rifled it of the poems that appear in "England's Helicon" and in the following pages.

In conclusion, the reader will remember that the present volume forms part of a series, which began with "Lyrics from Elizabethan Songbooks" and will end with Davison's "Poetical Rhapsody."

YELVERTON VILLAS, TWICKENHAM,
April, 1890.

INDEX OF FIRST LINES.

‘

INDEX OF FIRST LINES.

	PAGE
A BLITHE and bonny country lass (Lodge)	50
A seeing friend, yet enemy to rest (Phænix' Nest)	144
A turtle sat upon a leafless tree (Lodge)	47
Accurst be Love and those that trust his trains (Lodge)	133
Ah, poor conceit, delight is dead (Breton)	121
Ah, what is Love? It is a pretty thing (Greene)	22
And did not you hear of a mirth that befell (Friar Bacon)	61
As Love is cause of joy (Munday)	74
At shearing time she shall command (Breton)	112
Beauty sat bathing by a spring (Munday)	77
By your leave a little while (Breton)	99
Calling to mind mine eye long went about (Raleigh)	138
Children's Ahs and women's Ohs (Breton)	100
Come, all the world, submit yourselves to care (Breton)	57
Come, little babe, come, silly soul (Breton ?)	92
Cupid abroad was lated in the night (Greene)	21
Deceiving world, that with alluring toys (Greene)	40
Declare, O mind, from fond desires excluded (Phoenix' Nest)	141
Dildido, dildido (Greene)	32
Down a down! (Lodge)	48
Except I love I cannot have delight (Mirror of Knighthood)	63
Fain to content I bend myself to write (Lodge)	134
Fain would I have a pretty thing (Clement Robinson)	129
Fair Pastora, cease off delay (Mirror of Knighthood)	64
Farewell, Love and loving folly (Breton)	97
Fear not, faint heart, time may prove (Mirror of Knighthood)	73
Fie, fie on blind fancy (Greene)	39
First shall the heavens want starry light (Lodge)	43
Flora hath been all about (Breton)	107

PAGE

Fond feigning poets make of love a god (Greene) 20
For pity, pretty eyes, surcease (Lodge) 136
Fortune is blind, she looks on no man's need (Mirror of Knight-
    hood) 67

He that hath spent his time in silent moan (Munday) 77
He that was gotten in a Christmas night (Breton) 117
Heavenly fair Urania's son (Sheppard?) 86

I have neither plums nor cherries (Breton) 111
I smile to see how you devise (Clement Robinson) 127
I would I had as much as might be had (Breton) 117
I would thou wert not fair or I were wise (Breton) 58
If I must (sweet Love) obey (Mirror of Knighthood) 66
If that love had been a king (Breton) 98
Ill betide him that love seeks (Tofte) 79
In Cyprus sat fair Venus by a fount (Greene) 10
In time we see the silver drops (Greene) 9
It was a frosty winter-season (Greene) 35
It was a valley gaudy-green (Greene) 30

Let Mother-Earth now deck herself in flowers (Sidney) 5
Like to a top which runneth round (Brathwait) 85
Like to Diana in her summer-weed (Greene) 17
Love in my bosom like a bee (Lodge) 41
Love, leaving Heaven, gan post to Stygian lake (Dickenson) . . 53
Love resisted is a child (Mirror of Knighthood) 71
Love, what art thou? a vain thought (Lady Mary Wroth) . . 80
Lovely kind, and kindly loving (Breton) 101

Maid, will ye love me, yea or no? (Clement Robinson) 131
Mars, in a fury 'gainst Love's brightest Queen (Greene) . . . 19
Men talk of love that know not what it is (Breton) 105
My bonny lass, thine eye (Lodge) 136
My heart will burst except it be discharged (Mirror of Knighthood) 68
My true love hath my heart, and I have his (Sidney) 2

Nature, foreseeing how men would devise (Greene) 38
Now Christmas draweth near, and most men make good cheer
    (Breton) 89
Now sleep, and take thy rest (Mabbe) 83

O Night, O jealous Night, repugnant to my measures (Phœnix'
    Nest) 145
O words, which fall like summer dew on me (Sidney) 3

PAGE

Of all chaste birds the Phœnix doth excel (Lodge) 45

Oh my thoughts, keep in your words (Breton) 94

Oh, tired heart, too full of sorrows (Breton) 96

On women Nature did bestow two eyes (Greene) 38

Once I thought, but falsely thought (Mirror of Knighthood) . . 70

Phillis kept sheep along the western plains (Greene) 12

Phœbe sat (Lodge) 44

Phœbus, farewell! a sweeter Saint I serve (Sidney) . . . . ´ 1

Pluck the fruit and taste the pleasure (Lodge) 51

Pretty twinkling starry eyes (Breton) 115

Prove but as constant as th' art bold (George-a-Green) 61

Reason and duty both commandeth me (Munday) 76

She that is neither fair, nor rich, nor wise (Breton) 116

Sitting by a river's side (Greene) 34

Skin more pure than Ida's snow (Brathwait) 84

Some say Love (Greene) 14

Sweet Adon, dar'st not glance thine eye (Greene) 24

Sweet are the thoughts that savour of content (Greene) 33

Tell me, tell me, pretty muse (Breton) 114

That brow which doth with fair all fairs excel (Mirror of
   Knighthood) 72

The Christmas now is past, and I have kept my fast (Breton). . 90

The drops of rain in time the marble pierce (Greene) 63

The gentle season of the year (Phœnix' Nest) 140

The Siren Venus nouriced in her lap (Greene) 11

The time when first I fell in love (Phoenix' Nest) 139

The wealthy rascal, be he ne'er so base (Breton) 102

Though I be scorned, yet will I not disdain (Mirror of Knighthood) 65

To couple is a custom (Friar Bacon) 59

To make a truce, sweet Mistress, with your eyes (Phœnix' Nest) . 143

To see a strange outlandish fowl (Farley) 83

Trust not his wanton tears (Chettle) 78

Turn I my looks unto the skies (Lodge) 46

Weep not, my wanton, smile upon my knee (Greene) 15

What art thou, Will? (Breton) 55

Whate'er he is that would behold (Mirror of Knighthood) . . . 74

When gods had framed the sweet of women's face (Greene) . . 18

When lordly Saturn in a sable robe (Greene) 26

When tender ewes brought home with evening sun (Greene) . . . 16

Whenas the hunter goeth out (Clement Robinson) 125

	PAGE
Who can blame me if I love (Lady Mary Wroth)	81
Who can live in heart so glad (Breton)	108
Who doth desire that chaste his wife should be (Sidney)	8
Who thinks himself at freedom most of all (Mirror of Knighthood)	62
Why dost thou haste away (Sidney)	4
With sorrow, tears, and discontent (Young)	52
You birds whose warblings prove (Mabbe)	83

POEMS FROM ROMANCES AND PROSE-TRACTS.

PHŒBUS, FAREWELL!

PHŒBUS, farewell! a sweeter Saint I serve :
   The high conceits thy heav'nly wisdoms breed
My thoughts forget, my thoughts which never swerve
From her in whom is sown their freedom's seed,
And in whose eyes my daily doom I read.

Phœbus, farewell! a sweeter Saint I serve :
Thou art far off, thy kingdom is above ;
She heaven on earth with beauties doth preserve ;
Thy beams I like, but her clear rays I love ;
Thy force I fear, her force I still do prove.

Phœbus, yield up thy title in my mind :
She doth possess, thy image is defaced ;
But, if thy rage some brave revenge will find,
On her who hath in me thy temple raced
Employ thy might that she my fires may taste,
   And, how much more her worth surmounteth thee,
   Make her as much more base by loving me.

1 The poems that I have selected from Sidney's romance are
not found in the first edition (1590).

MY TRUE LOVE HATH MY HEART, AND I HAVE HIS.

M Y true love hath my heart, and I have his,
　　By just exchange one for the other given :
I hold his dear, and mine he can not miss ;
There never was a bargain better driven.
His heart in me keeps me and him in one ;
My heart in him his thoughts and senses guides :
He loves my heart for once it was his own ;
I cherish his because in me it bides.
His heart his wound received from my sight ;
My heart was wounded with his wounded heart :
For as from me on him his hurt did light,
So still methought in me his hurt did smart.
Both equal hurt, in this change sought our bliss :
My true love hath my heart, and I have his.

PROMISED WEAL.

O WORDS, which fall like summer dew on me!
 O breath, more sweet than is the growing bean!
O tongue, in which all honeyed liquors be!
O voice, that doth the thrush in shrillness stain!
  Do you say still this is her promise due:
  That she is mine, as I to her am true!

Gay hair, more gay than straw when harvest lies!
Lips, red and plump as cherries' ruddy side!
Eyes, fair and great, like fair great ox's eyes!
O breast, in which two white sheep swell in pride!
  Join you with me to seal this promise due:
  That she be mine, as I to her am true!

But thou, white skin, as white as curds well pressed,
So smooth as sleek-stone like it smoothes each part!
And thou, dear flesh, as soft as wool new dressed,
And yet as hard as brawn made hard by art!
  First four but say, next four their saying seal;
  But you must pay the gage of promised weal.

TITAN'S BRIGHTNESS STAINED.

WHY dost thou haste away,
    O Titan fair, the giver of the day?
Is it to carry news
To western wights what stars in east appear?
Or dost thou think that here
Is left a Sun whose beams thy place may use?
Yet stay, and well peruse
What be her gifts that make her equal thee ;
Bend all thy light to see
In earthly clothes enclosed a heavenly spark.
Thy running course cannot such beauties mark ;
No, no, thy motions be
Hastened from us with bar of shadow dark
Because that thou, the author of our sight,
Disdain'st we feel thee stained with other's light.

EPITHALAMIUM.

LET Mother Earth now deck herself in flowers,
To see her offspring seek a good increase,
Where justest love doth vanquish Cupid's powers,
And war of thoughts is swallowed up in peace,
Which never may decrease,
But, like the turtles fair,
Live one in two, a well-united pair :
Which that no chance may stain,
O Hymen ! long their coupled joys maintain !

O Heaven ! awake, show forth thy stately face ;
Let not these slumbering clouds thy beauties hide,
But with thy cheerful presence help to grace
The honest Bridegroom and the bashful Bride,
Whose loves may ever bide,
Like to the elm and vine,
With mutual embracements them to twine :
In which delightful pain,
O Hymen ! long their coupled joys maintain !

Ye Muses all ! which chaste affects allow
And have to Thyrsis shewed your secret skill,
To this chaste love your sacred favours bow ;
And so to him and her your gifts distill
That they all vice may kill
And, like to lilies pure,

May please all eyes, and spotless may endure :
   Where that all bliss may reign,
  O Hymen ! long their coupled joys maintain !

Ye Nymphs which in the waters empire have !
Since Thyrsis' music oft doth yield you praise,
Grant to the thing which we for Thyrsis crave :
Let one time—but long first—close up their days,
    One grave their bodies seize ;
    And, like two rivers sweet
  When they though divers do together meet,
    One stream both streams contain !
  O Hymen ! long their coupled joys maintain !

Pan ! father Pan, the god of silly sheep !
Whose care is cause that they in number grow,—
Have much more care of them that them do keep,
Since from these good the others' good doth flow ;
    And make their issue show
    In number like the herd
  Of younglings which thyself with love hast rear'd,
    Or like the drops of rain !
  O Hymen ! long their coupled joys maintain !

Virtue, if not a God, yet God's chief part !
Be thou the knot of this their open vow :
That still he be her head, she be his heart ;
He lean to her, she unto him do bow ;
    Each other still allow ;
    Like oak and mistletoe,
  Her strength from him, his praise from her do grow !
    In which most lovely train,
  O Hymen ! long their coupled joys maintain !

But thou, foul Cupid, sire to lawless lust !
Be thou far hence with thy empoisoned dart,
Which, though of glittering gold, shall here take rust
Where simple love, which chasteness doth impart,
  Avoids thy hurtful art,
  Not needing charming skill
 Such minds with sweet affections for to fill :
  Which being pure and plain,
 O Hymen ! long their coupled joys maintain !

All churlish words, shrewd answers, crabbed looks,
All privateness, self-seeking, inward spite,
All waywardness which nothing kindly brooks,
All strife for toys and claiming master's right,
  Be hence aye put to flight ;
  All stirring husband's hate
 'Gainst neighbours good for womanish debate
  Be fled, as things most vain !
 O Hymen ! long their coupled joys maintain !

All peacock pride and fruits of peacock's pride,
Longing to be with loss of substance gay,
With recklessness what may thy house betide
So that you may on higher slippers stay,
  For ever hence away !
  Yet let not sluttery,
 The sink of filth, be counted housewifery,
  But keeping wholesome mean !
 O Hymen ! long their coupled joys maintain !

But above all, away vile jealousy,
The evil of evils, just cause to be unjust !

How can he love, suspecting treachery?
How can she love, where love can not win trust?
     Go, snake! hide thee in dust;
     Nor dare once show thy face
   Where open hearts do hold so constant place
     That they thy sting restrain!
   O Hymen! long their coupled joys maintain!

The Earth is decked with flowers, the Heavens dis-
     played,
   Muses grant gifts, Nymphs long and joined life,
Pan store of babes, virtue their thoughts well stayed,
   Cupid's lust gone, and gone is bitter strife.
     Happy man! happy wife!
     No pride shall them oppress,
   Nor yet shall yield to loathsome sluttishness;
     And jealousy is slain,
   For Hymen will their coupled joys maintain.

TRUTH DOTH TRUTH DESERVE.

WHO doth desire that chaste his wife should be,
   First be he true, for truth doth truth deserve:
Then such be he as she his worth may see,
And one man still credit with her preserve.

Not toying kind, nor causelessly unkind;
Not stirring thoughts, nor yet denying right;
Not spying faults, nor in plain errors blind;
Never hard hand, nor ever reins too light.

As far from want as far from vain expense
(The one doth force, the latter doth entice) ;
Allow good company, but keep from thence
All filthy mouths that glory in their vice.
This done, thou hast no more, but leave the rest
To virtue, fortune, time and woman's breast.

From ROBERT GREENE'S *Arbasto*,
1584.

TIME.

IN time we see the silver drops
   The craggy stones make soft ;
The slowest snail in time we see
   Doth creep and climb aloft.

With feeble puffs the tallest pine
   In tract of time doth fall ;
The hardest heart in time doth yield
   To Venus' luring call.

Where chilling frost alate did nip,
   There flasheth now a fire ;
Where deep disdain bred noisome hate,
   There kindleth now desire.

Time causeth hope to have his hap :
   What care in time not eased ?
In time I loathed that now I love,
   In both content and pleased.

From *Perimedes the Blacksmith,*
1588.

WANTON YOUTH.

IN Cyprus sat fair Venus by a fount,
 Wanton Adonis toying on her knee :
She kissed the wag, her darling of account ;
 The boy gan blush ; which when his lover see,
She smiled, and told him love might challenge debt,
And he was young, and might be wanton yet.

The boy waxed bold, fired by fond desire,
 That woo he could and court her with conceit :
Reason spied this, and sought to quench the fire
 With cold disdain ; but wily Adon straight
Cheered up the flame, and said, " Good sir, what let ?
I am but young, and may be wanton yet."

Reason replied, that beauty was a bane
 To such as feed their fancy with fond love,
That when sweet youth with lust is overta'en,
 It rues in age : this could not Adon move,
For Venus taught him still this rest to set,
That he was young, and might be wanton yet.

Where Venus strikes with beauty to the quick,
 It little 'vails sage Reason to reply ;
Few are the cares for such as are love-sick,
 But love : then, though I wanton it awry,
And play the wag, from Adon this I get,—
I am but young, and may be wanton yet.

WANTON YOUTH REPROVED

THE Siren Venus nouriced [1] in her lap
    Fair Adon, swearing whiles he was a youth
He might be wanton : note his after-hap,
    The guerdon that such lawless lust ensu'th ;
So long he followed flattering Venus' lore,
Till, seely lad, he perished by a boar.

Mars in his youth did court this lusty dame,
    He won her love ; what might his fancy let ?
He was but young : at last, unto his shame,
    Vulcan entrapped them slyly in a net,
And called the gods to witness as a truth,
A lecher's fault was not excused by youth.

If crooked age accounteth youth his spring,
    The spring, the fairest season of the year,
Enriched with flowers, and sweets, and many a thing,
    That fair and gorgeous to the eyes appear ;
It fits that youth, the spring of man, should be
Riched with such flowers as virtue yieldeth thee.

[1] Nursed.

PHILLIS AND CORIDON.

PHILLIS kept sheep along the western plains,
    And Coridon did feed his flocks hard by :
This shepherd was the flower of all the swains
    That traced the downs of fruitful Thessaly ;
And Phillis, that did far her flocks surpass
In silver hue, was thought a bonny lass.

A bonny lass, quaint in her country 'tire,
    Was lovely Phillis, Coridon swore so ;
Her locks, her looks, did set the swain on fire,
    He left his lambs, and he began to woo ;
He looked, he sighed, he courted with a kiss,
No better could the silly swad [1] than this.

He little knew to paint a tale of love,
    Shepherds can fancy, but they cannot say :
Phillis gan smile, and wily thought to prove
    What uncouth [2] grief poor Coridon did pay ;
She asked him how his flocks or he did fare,
Yet pensive thus his sighs did tell his care.

The shepherd blushed when Phillis questioned so,
    And swore by Pan it was not for his flock[s] ;
" 'Tis love, fair Phillis, breedeth all this woe,
    My thoughts are trapt within thy lovely locks,

---

[1] Clown.   [2] Strange, unaccustomed.

Thine eye hath pierced, thy face hath set on fire ;
Fair Phillis kindleth Coridon's desire."

"Can shepherds love?" said Phillis to the swain.
"Such saints as Phillis," Coridon replied.
"Men when they lust can many fancies feign,"
Said Phillis.   This not Coridon denied,
That lust had lies ; "But love," quoth he, "says truth :
Thy shepherd loves, then, Phillis, what ensu'th?"

Phillis was won, she blushed and hung the head ;
The swain stept to, and cheered her with a kiss :
With faith, with troth, they struck the matter dead ;
So used they when men thought not amiss :
This love begun and ended both in one ;
Phillis was loved, and she liked Coridon.

From *Menaphon*, 1589.

IN LOVE'S DISPRAISE.

SOME say Love,
  Foolish Love,
    Doth rule and govern all the gods :
I say Love,
Inconstant Love,
    Sets men's senses far at odds.
Some swear Love,
Smooth-faced [1] Love,
    Is sweetest sweet that men can have :
I say Love,
Sour Love,
    Makes virtue yield as beauty's slave :
A bitter sweet, a folly worst of all,
That forceth wisdom to be folly's thrall.

Love is sweet :
Wherein sweet ?
    In fading pleasures that do pain.
Beauty sweet :
Is that sweet,
    That yieldeth sorrow for a gain ?
If Love's sweet,
Herein sweet,
    That minutes' joys are monthly woes :
'Tis not sweet,
That is sweet
    Nowhere but where repentance grows.
Then love who list, if beauty be so sour ;
Labour for me, Love rest in prince's bower.

[1] Old ed. " smooth'd face."

WEEP NOT, MY WANTON.

WEEP not, my wanton, smile upon my knee ;
　　When thou art old there's grief enough for thee.
　Mother's wag, pretty boy,
　Father's sorrow, father's joy ;
　When thy father first did see
　Such a boy by him and me,
　He was glad, I was woe ;
　Fortune changed made him so,
　When he left his pretty boy,
　Last his sorrow, first his joy.

Weep not, my wanton, smile upon my knee ;
When thou art old there's grief enough for thee.
　Streaming tears that never stint,
　Like pearl-drops from a flint,
　Fell by course from his eyes,
　That one another's place supplies ;
　Thus he grieved in every part,
　Tears of blood fell from his heart,
　When he left his pretty boy,
　Father's sorrow, father's joy.

Weep not, my wanton, smile upon my knee ;
When thou art old there's grief enough for thee.
　The wanton smiled, father wept,
　Mother cried, baby lept ;
　More he crowed, more we cried,
　Nature could not sorrow hide :
　He must go, he must kiss
　Child and mother, baby bliss,[1]
　For he left his pretty boy,
　Father's sorrow, father's joy.
Weep not, my wanton, smile upon my knee ;
When thou art old there's grief enough for thee.

[1] Bless.

THE EAGLE AND THE FLY.

WHEN tender ewes, brought home with evening sun,
  Wend to their folds,
  And to their holds
The shepherds trudge when light of day is done,
  Upon a tree
The eagle, Jove's fair bird, did perch ;
  There resteth he :
A little fly his harbour then did search,
And did presume, though others laughed thereat,
To perch whereas the princely eagle sat.

The eagle frowned, and shook his royal wings,
  And charged the fly
  From thence to hie :
Afraid, in haste the little creature flings,
  Yet seeks again,
Fearful, to perk him by the eagle's side :
  With moody vein,
The speedy post of Ganymede replied,
" Vassal, avaunt, or with my wings you die :
Is't fit an eagle seat him with a fly ? "

The fly craved pity, still the eagle frowned :
  The silly fly,
  Ready to die,
Disgraced, displaced, fell grovelling to the ground :
  The eagle saw,
And with a royal mind said to the fly,
  " Be not in awe,
I scorn by me the meanest creature die ;
Then seat thee here."   The joyful fly up flings,
And sat safe-shadowed with the eagle's wings.

DORON'S DESCRIPTION OF SAMELA.

L IKE to Diana in her summer-weed,
   Girt with a crimson robe of brightest dye,
          Goes fair Samela ;

Whiter than be the flocks that straggling feed,
When washed by Arethusa Fount [1] they lie,
          Is fair Samela ;

As fair Aurora in her morning-grey,
Decked with the ruddy glister of her love,
          Is fair Samela ;

Like lovely Thetis on a calmed day,
Whenas her brightness Neptune's fancy move,
          Shines fair Samela ;

Her tresses gold, her eyes like glassy streams,
Her teeth are pearl, the breasts are ivory
          Of fair Samela ;

Her cheeks, like rose and lily, yield forth gleams,
Her brows bright arches framed of ebony :
          Thus fair Samela

Passeth fair Venus in her bravest hue,
And Juno in the show of majesty,
          For she's Samela ;

Pallas in wit, all three, if you well view,
For beauty, wit, and matchless dignity,
          Yield to Samela.

[1] Sidney Walker's correction.—Old eds. "faint."

C

From *Ciceronis Amor*, 1589.

JEALOUSY.

WHEN gods had framed the sweet of women's
       face,
   And locked men's looks within their golden hair,
That Phœbus blushed to see their matchless grace,
   And heavenly gods on earth did make repair ;
To quip fair Venus' overweening pride,
Love's happy thoughts to jealousy were tied.

Then grew a wrinkle on fair Venus' brow ;
   The amber sweet of love is turned to gall ;
Gloomy was heaven ; bright Phœbus did avow
   He could be coy, and would not love at all,
Swearing, no greater mischief could be wrought
Than love united to a jealous thought.

VENUS VICTRIX.

M ARS in a fury 'gainst Love's brightest Queen,
    Put on his helm, and took him to his lance ;
On Erycinus [1] Mount was Mavors seen,
    And there his ensigns did the god advance,
And by heaven's greatest gates he stoutly swore,
Venus should die, for she had wronged him sore.

Cupid heard this, and he began to cry,
    And wished his mother's absence for a while :
" Peace, fool," quoth Venus ; "is it I must die ?
    Must it be, Mars ?" with that she coined a smile ;
She trimmed her tresses, and did curl her hair,
And made her face with beauty passing fair.

A fan of silver feathers in her hand,
    And in a coach of ebony she went :
She passed the place where furious Mars did stand,
    And out her looks a lovely smile she sent ;
Then from her brows leaped out so sharp a frown,
That Mars for fear threw all his armour down.

He vowed repentance for his rash misdeed,
    Blaming his choler that had caused his woe :
Venus grew gracious, and with him agreed,
    But charged him not to threaten beauty so,
For women's looks are such enchanting charms
As can subdue the greatest god in arms.

1 " Our author seems to forget here that the mountain, from
which Venus had the name of Erycina, was Eryx : it is not likely
that he wrote 'Erycina's *Mount.*'"—*Dyce.* In GREENE'S *Orpha-*
rion the form " Erycinus" occurs several times ; *e.g.* " I crave so
much favour at thy hands as to tell me whether Venus is resident
about this Mount of *Erycinus* or no."

LOVE SCHOOLED.

FOND, feigning poets make of love a god,
   And leave the laurel for the myrtle-boughs
When Cupid is a child not past the rod,
   And fair Diana Daphne [1] most allows :
I'll wear the bays, and call the wag a boy,
And think of love but as a foolish toy.

Some give him bow and quiver at his back,
   Some make him blind to aim without advice,
When, naked wretch, such feathered bolts he lack
   And sight he hath, but cannot wrong the wise ;
For use but labour's weapon for defence,
And Cupid, like a coward, flieth thence.

He's god in court, but cottage calls him child,
   And Vesta's virgins with their holy fires
Do cleanse the thoughts that fancy hath defiled,
   And burn the palace of his fond desires ;
With chaste disdain they scorn the foolish god,
And prove him but a boy not past the rod.

[1] Old ed. " Daphnis."

From *The Orpharion*, licensed in
1589.

LOVE'S TREACHERY.

CUPID [1] abroad was lated in the night,
 His wings were wet with ranging in the rain ;
Harbour he sought, to me he took his flight,
 To dry his plumes : I heard the boy complain ;
  I oped the door, and granted his desire,
  I rose myself, and made the wag a fire.

Looking more narrow by the fire's flame,
 I spied his quiver hanging by his back :
Doubting the boy might my misfortune frame,
 I would have gone for fear of further wrack ;
  But what I drad, did me poor wretch betide,
  For forth he drew an arrow from his side.

He pierced the quick, and I began to start,
 A pleasing wound, but that it was too high ;
His shaft procured a sharp, yet sugared smart :
 Away he flew, for why [2] his wings were dry ;
  But left the arrow sticking in my breast,
  That sore I grieved I welcomed such a guest.

[1] These verses (after Anacreon), with some textual variations,
are also found in Greene's *Alcida*, licensed in 1588.
[2] " For why " = because.

From *The Mourning Garment,*
1590.

THE SHEPHERDS WIFE'S SONG.

A H, what is love?   It is a pretty thing,
　　As sweet unto a shepherd as a king ;
　　　　And sweeter too,
For kings have cares that wait upon a crown,
And cares can make the sweetest love to frown :
　　　　Ah then, ah then,
If country loves such sweet desires do gain,
What lady would not love a shepherd swain?

His flocks are folded, he comes home at night,
As merry as a king in his delight ;
　　　　And merrier too,
For kings bethink them what the state require,
Where shepherds careless carol by the fire :
　　　　Ah then, ah then,
If country loves such sweet desires do gain,
What lady would not love a shepherd swain?

He kisseth first, then sits as blithe to eat
His cream and curds as doth the king his meat ;
　　　　And blither too,
For kings have often fears when they do sup,
Where shepherds dread no poison in their cup :
　　　　Ah then, ah then,
If country loves such sweet desires do gain,
What lady would not love a shepherd swain?

To bed he goes, as wanton then, I ween,
As is a king in dalliance with a queen ;
   More wanton too,
For kings have many griefs affects to move,
Where shepherds have no greater grief than love :
   Ah then, ah then,
If country loves such sweet desires do gain,
What lady would not love a shepherd swain?

Upon his couch of straw he sleeps as sound,
As doth the king upon his beds of down ;
   More sounder too,
For cares cause kings full oft their sleep to spill,
Where weary shepherds lie and snort their fill :
   Ah then, ah then,
If country loves such sweet desires do gain,
What lady would not love a shepherd swain ?

Thus with his wife he spends the year, as blithe
As doth the king at every tide or sithe ; [1]
   And blither too,
For kings have wars and broils to take in hand,
Where shepherds laugh and love upon the land :
   Ah then, ah then,
If country loves such sweet desires do gain,
What lady would not love a shepherd swain ?

[1] Time.

From *Never too Late,* 1590.

N'OSEREZ VOUS, MON BEL AMI?

SWEET Adon, darest not glance thine eye—
   N'oserez vous, mon bel ami?—
Upon thy Venus that must die?
   Je vous en prie, pity me ;
N'oserez vous, mon bel, mon bel,
N'oserez vous, mon bel ami?

See how sad thy Venus lies,—
   N'oserez vous, mon bel ami?—
Love in heart, and tears in eyes ;
   Je vous en prie, pity me ;
N'oserez vous, mon bel, mon bel,
N'oserez vous, mon bel ami?

Thy face as fair as Paphos' brooks,—
   N'oserez vous, mon bel ami? —
Wherein fancy baits her hooks ;
   Je vous en prie, pity me ;
N'oserez vous, mon bel, mon bel,
N' oserez vous, mon bel ami?

Thy cheeks like cherries that do grow—
   N'oserez vous, mon bel, ami?—
Amongst the western mounts of snow ;
   Je vous en prie, pity me ;
N'oserez vous, mon bel, mon bel,
N' oserez vous, mon bel ami?

Thy lips vermilion, full of love,—
  N'oserez vous, mon bel ami ?—
Thy neck as silver-white as dove ;
  Je vous en prie, pity me ;
N'oserez vous, mon bel, mon bel,
N'oserez vous, mon bel ami?

Thine eyes, like flames of holy fires,—
  N'oserez vous, mon bel ami ?—
Burn all my thoughts with sweet desires ;
  Je vous en prie, pity me ;
N'oserez vous, mon bel, mon bel,
N'oserez vous, mon bel ami?

All thy beauties sting my heart ;—
  N'oserez vous, mon bel ami ?—
I must die through Cupid's dart;
  Je vous en prie, pity me ;
N'oserez vous, mon bel, mon bel,
N'oserez vous, mon bel ami ?

Wilt thou let thy Venus die ?—
  N'oserez vous, mon bel ami ?—
Adon were unkind, say I,—
  Je vous en prie, pity me ;
N'oserez vous, mon bel, mon bel,
N'oserez vous, mon bel ami?

To let fair Venus die for woe—
  N'oserez vous, mon bel ami ?—
That doth love sweet Adon so ;
  Je vous en prie, pity me ;
N'oserez vous, mon bel, mon bel,
N'oserez vous, mon bel ami?

From *Francesco's Fortunes ; or
the Second Part of Never
Too Late,* 1590.

EURYMACHUS' FANCY IN THE PRIME OF HIS AFFECTION.

WHEN lordly Saturn, in a sable robe,
    Sat full of frowns and mourning in the west,
The evening-star scarce peeped from out her lodge,
And Phœbus newly gallopped to his rest ;
          Even then
          Did I
Within my boat sit in the silent streams,
All void of cares as he that lies and dreams.

As Phao, so a ferryman I was ;
The country-lasses said I was too fair :
With easy toil I laboured at mine oar,
To pass from side to side who did repair ;
          And then
          Did I
For pains take pence, and Charon-like transport
As soon the swain as men of high import.

When want of work did give me leave to rest,
My sport was catching of the wanton fish :
So did I wear the tedious time away,
And with my labour mended oft my dish ;

For why [1]
I thought
That idle hours were calendars of ruth,
And time ill-spent was prejudice to youth.

I scorned to love ; for were the nymph as fair
As she that loved the beauteous Latmian swain,
Her face, her eyes, her tresses, nor her brows
Like ivory, could my affection gain ;
For why
I said
With high disdain, " Love is a base desire,
And Cupid's flames, why, they're but watery fire."

As thus I sat, disdaining of proud Love,
" Have over, ferryman," there cried a boy ;
And with him was a paragon for hue,
A lovely damsel, beauteous and coy ;
And there
With her
A maiden, covered with a tawny veil,
Her face unseen for breeding lovers' bale.

I stirred [2] my boat, and when I came to shore,
The boy was winged ; methought it was a wonder ;
The dame had eyes like lightning, or the flash
That runs before the hot report of thunder ;
Her smiles
Were sweet,
Lovely her face ; was ne'er so fair a creature,
For earthly carcass had a heavenly feature.

[1] " For why " = because.   [2] Steered.

" My friend," quoth she, "sweet ferryman, behold,
We three must pass, but not a farthing fare ;
But I will give, for I am Queen of love,
The brightest lass thou lik'st unto thy share ;
        Choose where
        Thou lov'st,
Be she as fair as Love's sweet lady is,
She shall be thine, if that will be thy bliss."

With that she smiled with such a pleasing face
As might have made the marble rock relent ;
But I, that triumphed in disdain of love,
Bade fie on him that to fond love was bent,
        And then
        Said thus,
" So light the ferryman for love doth care,
As Venus pass not if she pay no fare."

At this a frown sat on her angry brow ;
She winks upon her wanton son hard by ;
He from his quiver drew a bolt of fire,
And aimed so right as that he pierced mine eye ;
        And then
        Did she
Draw down the veil that hid the virgin's face,
Whose heavenly beauty lightened all the place.

Straight then I leaned mine ear upon mine arm,
And looked upon the nymph (if so) was fair ;
Her eyes were stars, and like Apollo's locks
Methought appeared the trammels of her hair :

Thus did
I gaze
And sucked in beauty, till that sweet desire
Cast fuel on, and set my thought on fire.

When I was lodged within the net of love,
And that they saw my heart was all on flame,
The nymph away, and with her trips along
The winged boy, and with her goes his dame :
O, then
I cried,
" Stay, ladies, stay, and take not any care,
You all shall pass, and pay no penny fare."

Away they fling, and looking coyly back,
They laugh at me, O, with a loud disdain !
I send out sighs to overtake the nymph,[1]
And tears, as lures, to call them back again ;
But they
Fly thence ;
But I sit in my boat, with hand on oar,
And feel a pain, but know not what's the sore.

At last I feel it is the flame of love,
I strive, but bootless, to express the pain ;
It cools, it fires, it hopes, it fears, it frets,
And stirreth passions throughout every vein ;
That down
I sat,
And sighing did fair Venus' laws approve,
And swore no thing so sweet and sour as love.

[1] Old ed. " Nimphs."

RADAGON IN DIANAM.

IT was a valley gaudy-green,
　Where Dian at the fount was seen ;
　　　Green it was,
　　　And did pass
All other of Diana's bowers
In the pride of Flora's flowers.

A fount it was that no sun sees,
Circled in with cypress-trees,
　　　Set so nigh
　　　As Phœbus' eye
Could not do the virgins scathe,
To see them naked when they bathe.

She sat there all in white,
Colour fitting her delight :
　　　Virgins so
　　　Ought to go,
· For white in armory is plac'd
To be the colour that is chaste.

Her taff'ta cassock might you see
Tucked up above her knee,
　　　Which did show
　　　There below
Legs as white as whalés-bone ;
So white and chaste were never none.

Hard by her, upon the ground,
Sat her virgins in a round,
  Bathing their
  Golden hair,
And singing all in notes high,
" Fie on Venus' flattering eye !

" Fie on love ! it is a toy ;
Cupid witless and a boy ;
  All his fires,
  And desires,
Are plagues that God sent down from high
To pester men with misery."

As thus the virgins did disdain
Lovers' joy and lovers' pain,
  Cupid nigh
  Did espy,
Grieving at Diana's song,
Slyly stole these maids among.

His bow of steel, darts of fire,
He shot amongst them sweet desire,
  Which straight flies
  In their eyes,
And at the entrance made them start,
For it ran from eye to heart.

Calisto straight supposed Jove
Was fair and frolic for to love ;
  Dian she
  Scaped not free,
For, well I wot, hereupon
She loved the swain Endymion ;

Clytie Phœbus, and Chloris' eye
Thought none so fair as Mercury :
       Venus thus
       Did discuss
By her son in darts of fire,
None so chaste to check desire.

Dian rose with all her maids,
Blushing thus at love's braids : [1]
       With sighs, all
       Show their thrall ;
And flinging hence pronounce this saw,
"What so strong as love's sweet law?"

MULLIDOR'S MADRIGAL.

DILDIDO, dildido,
    O love, O love,
I feel thy rage rumble below and above !

In summer-time I saw a face,
    Trop belle pour moi, hélas, hélas !
Like to a stoned-horse was her pace :
    Was ever young man so dismayed ?
Her eyes, like wax-torches, did make me afraid :
    Trop belle pour moi, voilà mon trépas.

---

[1] "*I.e.*, perhaps,—crafts, deceits (vide Steevens's note on "Since Frenchmen are so *braid.*" Shakespeare's *All well that ends well*, Act iv. sc. 2.)."—*Dyce.*

Thy beauty, my love, exceedeth supposes ;
Thy hair is a nettle for the nicest roses.
    Mon dieu, aide moi !
That I with the primrose of my fresh wit
May tumble her tyranny under my feet :
    Hé donc je serai un jeune roi !
Trop belle pour moi, hélas, hélas,
Trop belle pour moi, voilà mon trépas.

From *The Farewell to Folly*,
1591.

A MIND CONTENT.

SWEET are the thoughts that savour of content ;
    The quiet mind is richer than a crown ;
Sweet are the nights in careless slumber spent ;
    The poor estate scorns fortune's angry frown :
Such sweet content, such minds, such sleep, such bliss,
Beggars enjoy, when princes oft do miss.

The homely house that harbours quiet rest ;
    The cottage that affords no pride nor care ;
The mean that 'grees with country music best ;
    The sweet consort of mirth and music's [1] fare ;
Obscured life sets down a type of bliss :
A mind content both crown and kingdom is.

---

[1] " Music's fare " is hardly intelligible.—Mr. W. J. Linton
(*Rare Poems*) reads " modest fare."

From *Philomela, the Lady Fitz-
water's Nightingale,* 1592.

PHILOMELA'S ODE THAT SHE SUNG IN HER ARBOUR.

SITTING by a river's side,
　Where a silent stream did glide,
Muse I did of many things
That the mind in quiet brings.
I gan think how some men deem.
Gold their god ; and some esteem
Honour is the chief content
That to man in life is lent ;
And some others do contend,
Quiet none like to a friend ;
Others hold, there is no wealth
Compared to a perfect health ;
Some man's mind in quiet stands
When he is lord of many lands :
But I did sigh, and said all this
Was but a shade of perfect bliss ;
And in my thoughts I did approve,
Naught so sweet as is true love.
Love 'twixt lovers passeth these,
When mouth kisseth and heart 'grees,
With folded arms and lips meeting,
Each soul another sweetly greeting ;
For by the breath the soul fleeteth,
And soul with soul in kissing meeteth.

If love be so sweet a thing,
That such happy bliss doth bring,
Happy is love's sugared thrall ;
But unhappy maidens all,
Who esteem your virgin blisses
Sweeter than a wife's sweet kisses.
No such quiet to the mind
As true love with kisses kind :
But if a kiss prove unchaste,
Then is true love quite disgrac'd.
Though love be sweet, learn this of me
No love sweet but honesty.

PHILOMELA'S SECOND ODE.

IT was frosty winter-season,
  And fair Flora's wealth was geason.[1]
Meads that erst with green were spread,
With choice flowers diap'red,
Had tawny veils ; cold had scanted
What the spring and nature planted.
Leafless boughs there might you see,
All except fair Daphne's tree :
On their twigs no birds perched ;
Warmer coverts now they searched ;
And by nature's secret reason,
Framed their voices to the season,

[1] Rare, uncommon.

With their feeble tunes bewraying
How they grieved the spring's decaying.
Frosty winter thus had gloomed
Each fair thing that summer bloomed ;
Fields were bare, and trees unclad,
Flowers withered, birds were sad :
When I saw a shepherd fold
Sheep in cote, to shun the cold.
Himself sitting on the grass,
That with frost withered was,
Sighing deeply, thus gan say ;
" Love is folly when astray :
Like to love no passion such,
For 'tis madness, if too much ;
If too little, then despair ;
If too high, he beats the air
With bootless cries ; if too low,
An eagle matcheth with a crow :
Thence grow jars.   Thus I find,
Love is folly, if unkind ;
Yet do men most desire
To be heated with this fire,
Whose flame is so pleasing hot,
That they burn, yet feel it not.
Yet hath love another kind,
Worse than these unto the mind ;
That is, when a wanton eye
Leads desire clean awry,
And with the bee doth rejoice
Every minute to change choice,
Counting he were then in bliss,
If that each fair face were his.
Highly thus is love disgrac'd,

When the lover is unchaste,
And would taste of fruit forbidden,
'Cause the scape is easily hidden.
Though such love be sweet in brewing,
Bitter is the end ensuing ;
For the honour of love he shameth,
And himself with lust defameth ;
For a minute's pleasure gaining,
Fame and honour ever staining.
Gazing thus so far awry,
Last the chip falls in his eye ;
Then it burns that erst but heat him,
And his own rod gins to beat him ;
His choicest sweets turn to gall ;
He finds lust his sin's thrall ;
That wanton women in their eyes
Men's deceivings do comprise ;
That homage done to fair faces
Doth dishonour other graces.
If lawless love be such a sin,
Cursed is he that lives therein,
For the gain of Venus' game
Is the downfall unto shame."
Here he paused, and did stay ;
Sighed, and rose, and went away.

SONNET.

O N women Nature did bestow two eyes,
    Like heaven's bright lamps, in matchless beauty
      shining,
Whose beams do soonest captivate the wise,
And wary heads, made rare by art's refining.
But why did Nature, in her choice combining,
 Plant two fair eyes within a beauteous face,
That they might favour two with equal grace?
Venus did soothe up Vulcan with one eye,
With th' other granted Mars his wished glee :
If she did so who Hymen did defy,
Think love no sin, but grant an eye to me ;
In vain else Nature gave two stars to thee :
If then two eyes may well two friends maintain,
Allow of two, and prove not Nature vain.

ANSWER.

N ATURE foreseeing how men would devise
    More wiles than Proteus, women to entice,
Granted them two, and those bright-shining eyes,
To pierce into men's faults if they were wise ;
For they with show of virtue mask their vice :
Therefore to women's eyes belong these gifts,
The one must love, the other see men's shifts.
Both these await upon one simple heart,
And what they choose, it hides up without change.
The emerald will not with his portrait part,
Nor will a woman's thoughts delight to range ;
They hold it bad to have so bad exchange :   [him,
One heart, one friend, though that two eyes do choose
No more but one, and heart will never lose him.

From *The Groatsworth of Wit
bought with a Million of
Repentance*, 1592.

LAMILIA'S SONG.

FIE, fie on blind fancy !
    It hinders youth's joy :
Fair virgins, learn by me
To count Love a toy.
When Love learned first the A B C of delight,
And knew no figures nor conceited phrase,
He simply gave to due desert her right,
He led not lovers in dark winding ways ;
He plainly willed to love, or flatly answered no :
But now who lists to prove, shall find it'nothing so.
        Fie, fie, then, on fancy !
        It hinders youth's joy :
.   Fair virgins, learn by me
        To count love a toy.
For since he learned to use the poet's pen,
He learned likewise with smoothing words to feign,
Witching chaste ears with trothless tongues of men,
And wronged faith with falsehood and disdain.
He gives a promise now, anon he sweareth no :
Who listeth for to prove, shall find his changing so.
        Fie, fie, then, on fancy !
        It hinders youth's joy :
        Fair virgins, learn by me
        To count Love a toy.

MISERRIMUS.

DECEIVING world, that with alluring toys
　　Hast made my life the subject of thy scorn,
And scornest now to lend thy fading joys
T' outlength my life, whom friends have left forlorn ;
How well are they that die ere they be born,
　　And never see thy sleights, which few men shun
　　Till unawares they helpless are undone !

Oft have I sung of Love and of his fire ;
But now I find that poet was advised,
Which made full feasts increasers of desire,
And proves weak Love was with the poor despised ;
For when the life with food is not sufficed,
　　What thoughts of love, what motion of delight,
　　What pleasance can proceed from such a wight ?

Witness my want, the murderer of my wit :
My ravished sense, of wonted fury reft,
Wants such conceit as should in poems fit
Set down the sorrow wherein I am left :
But therefore have high heavens their gifts bereft,
　　Because so long they lent them me to use,
　　And I so long their bounty did abuse.

O, that a year were granted me to live,
And for that year my former wits restored !
What rules of life, what counsel would I give,
How should my sin with sorrow be deplored ! [1]
But I must die of every man abhorred :
　　Time loosely spent will not again be won ;
　　My time is loosely spent, and I undone.

　　　　[1] Dyce's correction.—Old ed. " then deplore."

From THOMAS LODGE'S *Rosalind*, 1590.

ROSALIND'S MADRIGAL.

LOVE in my bosom like a bee
   Doth suck his sweet ;
Now with his wings he plays with me,
   Now with his feet.
Within mine eyes he makes his nest,
His bed amidst my tender breast ;
My kisses are his daily feast,
And yet he robs me of my rest.
   Ah wanton, will ye ?

And if I sleep, then percheth he,
   With pretty flight,
And makes his pillow of my knee
   The livelong night.
Strike I my lute, he tunes the string ;
He music plays if so I sing ;
He lends me every lovely thing ;
Yet cruel he my heart doth sting.
   Whist, wanton, still ye !

Else I with roses every day
   Will whip you hence,
And bind you, when you long to play,
   For your offence.

I'll shut mine eyes to keep you in,
I'll make you fast it for your sin,
I'll count your power not worth a pin.
Alas, what hereby shall I win,
 If he gainsay me ?

What if I beat the wanton boy
 With many a rod?
He will repay me with annoy,
 Because a god.
Then sit thou safely on my knee,
Then let thy bower my bosom be ;
Lurk in mine eyes, I like of thee.
O Cupid, so thou pity me,
 Spare not, but play thee.

THE LOVER'S VOW.

FIRST shall the heavens want starry light,
  The seas be robbed of their waves ;
The day want sun, and sun want bright,
The night want shade, the dead men graves ;
    The April flowers and leaf and tree,
    Before I false my faith to thee.

First shall the tops of highest hills
By humble plains be overpried ;
And poets scorn the Muses' quills,
And fish forsake the water-glide ;
    And Iris lose her coloured weed,
    Before I fail thee at thy need.

First direful hate shall turn to peace,
And love relent in deep disdain ;
And death his fatal stroke shall cease,
And envy pity every pain ;
    And pleasure mourn, and sorrow smile,
    Before I talk of any guile.

First time shall stay his stayless race,
And winter bless his boughs with corn ;
And snow bemoisten July's face,
And winter spring, and summer mourn,
    Before my pen by help of fame
    Cease to recite thy sacred name.

MONTANUS' SONNET.

PHŒBE sat,
  Sweet she sat,
    Sweet sat Phœbe when I saw her,
White her brow,
Coy her eye ;
  Brow and eye how much you please me !
Words I spent,
Sighs I sent ;
  Sighs and words could never draw her.
Oh my love,
Thou art lost,
  Since no sight could ever ease thee.

Phœbe sat
By a fount,
  Sitting by a fount I spied her :
Sweet her touch,
Rare her voice :
  Touch and voice what may distain you ?
As she sang,
I did sigh,
  And by sighs whilst that I tried her,
Oh mine eyes !
You did lose
  Her first sight, whose want did pain you.

Phœbe's flocks,
White as wool,
   Yet were Phœbe's locks more whiter.
Phœbe's eyes
Dovelike mild,
   Dovelike eyes, both mild and cruel ;
Montan swears,
In your lamps
   He will die for to delight her.
Phœbe, yield,
Or I die :
   Shall true hearts be fancy's fuel ?

PRAISE OF ROSALIND.

OF all chaste birds the Phœnix doth excel,
  Of all strong beasts the lion bears the bell,
Of all sweet flowers the rose doth sweetest smell,
Of all fair maids my Rosalind is fairest.

Of all pure metals gold is only purest,
Of all high trees the pine hath highest crest,
Of all soft sweets I like my mistress' breast,
Of all chaste thoughts my mistress' thoughts are rarest.

Of all proud birds the eagle pleaseth Jove,
Of pretty fowls kind Venus likes the dove,
Of trees Minerva doth the olive love,
Of all sweet nymphs I honour Rosalind.

Of all her gifts her wisdom pleaseth most,
Of all her graces virtue she doth boast :
For all these gifts my life and joy is lost,
If Rosalind prove cruel and unkind.

TURN I MY LOOKS UNTO THE SKIES.

TURN I my looks unto the skies,
    Love with his arrows wounds mine eyes ;
If so I gaze upon the ground,
Love then in every flower is found ;
Search I the shade to fly my pain,
He meets me in the shade again ;
Wend I to walk in secret grove,
Ev'n there I meet with sacred Love ;
If so I bain me in the spring,
Ev'n on the brink I hear him sing ;
If so I meditate alone,
He will be partner of my moan ;
If so I mourn, he weeps with me,
And where I am there will he be.
Whenas I talk of Rosalind
The god from coyness waxeth kind,
And seems in self-same flames to fry
Because he loves as well as I.
Sweet Rosalind, for pity rue,
For why [1] than Love I am more true :
He, if he speed, will quickly fly,
But in thy love I live and die.

[1] " For why " — because.

MONTANUS' SONNET.

A TURTLE sat upon a leafless tree,
 Mourning her absent pheer,[1]
 With sad and sorry cheer :
 About her wondering stood
 The citizens of wood,
 And whilst her plumes she rents,
 And for her love laments,
 The stately trees complain them,
 The birds with sorrow pain them :
 Each one that doth her view,
 Her pain and sorrows rue :
 But were the sorrows known
 That me hath overthrown,
Oh how would Phœbe sigh, if she did look on me ?

The lovesick Polypheme that could not see,
 Who on the barren shore,
 His fortunes doth deplore,
 And melteth all in moan
 For Galatea gone ;
 And with his piteous cries,
 Afflicts both earth and skies,
 And to his woe betook,
 Doth break both pipe and hook :

[1] Mate.

For whom complains the morn,
For whom the Sea Nymphs mourn :
Alas, his pain is nought ;
For were my woe but thought,
Oh how would Phœbe sigh, if she did look on me ?

Beyond compare my pain :
    Yet glad am I,
If gentle Phœbe deign
    To see her Montan die.

PHŒBE'S SONNET, A REPLY TO MONTANUS' PASSION.

" DOWN a down !"
    Thus Phyllis sung
By fancy once distressed :
" Whoso by foolish loves are stung,
    Are worthily oppressed,
        And so sing I.   With a down, down !"

" When love was first begot,
    And by the mother's [1] will
Did fall to human lot
    His solace to fulfil,
Devoid of all deceit
    A chaste and holy fire
Did quicken man's conceit,
    And women's breasts inspire.

---

1 So ed. 1609 (and *England's Helicon*).—Earlier eds.
" mooucrs."

The gods that saw the good
  That mortals did approve,
With kind and holy mood,
  Began to talk of love.

  " Down a down !"
    Thus Phyllis sung
      By fancy once distressed, etc.

But during this accord,
  A wonder strange to hear :
Whilst love in deed and word
  Most faithful did appear,
False semblance came in place,
  By jealousy attended,
And with a double face
  Both love and fancy blended.
Which makes the gods forsake,
  And men from fancy fly,
And maidens scorn a make,[1]
  Forsooth and so will I.

  " Down a down !"
    Thus Phyllis sung
      By fancy once distressed :
  " Who so by foolish love are stung
    Are worthily oppressed.
And so sing I, with down, a down, a down a."

[1] " Make "—an old form of *mate*.

CORYDON'S SONG.

A BLITHE and bonny country lass,
 Heigh ho, the bonny lass :
Sat sighing on the tender grass,
 And weeping said, " Will none come woo me ?"
A smicker boy, a lither swain,
 Heigh ho, a smicker swain,
That in his love was wanton fain,
 With smiling looks straight came unto her.

When as the wanton wench espied,
 Heigh ho, when she espied,
The means to make herself a bride,
 She simpered smooth like bonnybell :
The swain that saw her squint-eyed kind,
 Heigh ho, squint-eyed kind,
His arms about her body twined,
 And "Fair lass, how fare ye well ?"

The country kit said " Well forsooth,
 Heigh ho, well forsooth ;
But that I have a longing tooth,
 A longing tooth that makes me cry."
" Alas !" said he, "what gars thy grief ?
 Heigh ho, what gars thy grief ?"
" A wound," quoth she, " without relief :
 I fear a maid that I shall die."

" If that be all," the shepherd said,
    " Heigh ho," the shepherd said,
" I'll make thee wive it, gentle maid,
    And so recure thy malady."

Hereon they kissed with many an oath,
    Heigh ho, with many an oath,
And 'fore God Pan did plight their troth,
    And to the church they hied them fast.

And God send every pretty peat,
    Heigh ho, the pretty peat,
That fears to die of this conceit,
    So kind a friend to help at last.

> From *The famous, true, and
> historical life of Robert,
> second Duke of Normandy,*
> 1591.

WHILST YOUTHFUL SPORTS ARE LASTING.

PLUCK the fruit and taste the pleasure,
    Youthful Lordings, of delight ;
Whilst occasion gives you seizure,
    Feed your fancies and your sight :
        After death, when you are gone,
        Joy and pleasure is there none.

Here on earth nothing is stable,
    Fortune's changes well are known ;
Whilst as youth doth then enable,
    Let your seeds of joy be sown :
        After death, when you are gone,
        Joy and pleasure is there none.

Feast it freely with your lovers,
  Blithe and wanton sports do fade,
Whilst that lovely Cupid hovers
  Round about this lovely shade :
    Sport it freely one to one,
    After death is pleasure none,

Now the pleasant spring allureth,
  And both place and time invites :
But, alas, what heart endureth
  To disclaim his sweet delights?
    After death, when we are gone,
    Joy and pleasure is there none.

From BARTHOLOMEW YOUNG'S
Diana of George of Monte-
mayor, 1598.[1]

LOVE'S SUSTENANCE.

WITH sorrow, tears, and discontent
  Love his forces doth augment.

Water is to meads delight,
And the flax doth please the fire ;
Oil in lamp agreeth right ;
Green meads are all the flocks' desire ;
Ripening fruit and wheaty ears
With due heat are well content ;
And with pains and many tears
Love his forces doth augment.

1 Young completed his translation of the Spanish romance in
1583. I have given only one brief specimen of the poetry. If
the reader is interested in Young's verse, I refer him to *England's
Helicon* (where he will find more than enough of it).

From JOHN DICKENSON'S *Aris-
bas, Euphues amidst his
slumbers,* 1594.

CUPID'S JOURNEY TO HELL.

L OVE, leaving heaven, 'gan post to Stygian lake,
  And, being landed on the farther shore,
For Pluto's palace did his journey make,
To view his uncle's court and royal store.

Thus, having crept from mother's side by stealth,
He welcomed is with pomp by bloodless ghosts ;
And hell's grim tyran,[1] greeting him with health,
His royalties to powerful nephew boasts.

Having viewed each strange hue of monstrous shape,
They feasted with great jollity in hell ;
And sauced their meat with store óf pressed grape,
Till wine did wit and sense from them expel.

Sleep, caused by fumes to their o'ercharged brains,
Did seize on both ; first Pluto took a nap ;
Next Cupid (thus his quaffing mood constrains)
Lay down to rest him, dreading no mishap.

In haste the fondling from his shoulders threw
His dear-bought quiver and his fatal bow :
Fair Proserpine came in, and at the view
Forthwith exclaimed, "These, these have wrought my
      woe !

---

[1] An old form of *tyrant.*

These, these caused me (deprived of wonted joy)
T'inhabit Hell ; these fired the lecher's lust :
But sith they are misguided by a boy,
I will commit them to another's trust."

This said, came Plutus headlong tumbling in,
Plutus the god of coin, blind as the other ;
Whom, with fair words the guileful queen did win
T'usurp those gifts and seem Love's second brother.

At first he feared, at last he was delighted
With using them, and smiled oft to think
How men's affections, by those shafts excited,
Obeyed his doom, which love with gold did link.

Cupid awaking missed the dreaded signs
Of godhead's might ; strange passions did him toss ;
He wreathes his arms in folds and them untwines,
Thus childishly he moans his hapless loss.

He wept, he fled, in hell he durst not hide him,
Grieved with the murmur of so many souls ;
Near heaven he dares not come lest Venus chide him
What should he do whom Fortune thus controuls ?

Foul fall the wag that lost so rare a jewel !
Long may he lurk, that could no better guard
His father's toil, his mother's pride, the fuel
Which for hearts' wracks eyes' glances have prepared !

> Sith then the god of gain usurps Love's room,
> I will with gifts make suit for gracious doom.

From NICHOLAS BRETON'S *The Will of Wit; Wit's Will, or Will's Wit, Chuse you Whether,* 1599.

A SONG BETWEEN WIT AND WILL.

Wit.

WHAT art thou, Will? *Will.* A babe of Nature's brood.

Wit. Who was thy sire? *Will.* Sweet Lust, as lovers say.

Wit. Thy mother who? *Will.* Wild lusty wanton blood.

Wit. When wert thou born? *Will.* In merry month of May.

Wit. And where brought up? *Will.* In school of little skill.

Wit. What learn'dst thou there? *Will.* Love is my lesson still.

Wit. Where read'st thou that? *Will.* In lines of sweet delight.

Wit. The author who? *Will.* Desire did draw the book.

Wit. Who teacheth? *Will.* Time. *Wit.* What order? *Will.* Lovers' right.

Wit. What's that? *Will.* To catch content by hook or crook.

Wit. Where keeps he school? *Will.* In wilderness of woe.

Wit. Why lives he there? *Will.* The Fates appoint it so.

Wit. Why did they so? *Will.* It was their secret will.

Wit. What was their will? *Will.* To work fond lovers woe.

Wit. What was their woe? *Will.* By spite their sport to spill.

Wit. What was their sport? *Will.* Dame Nature best doth know.

Wit. How grows their spite? *Will.* By want of wish. *Wit.* What's that?

Will. Wit knows right well, Will may not tell thee what.

Wit. Then, Will, adieu. *Will.* Yet stand me in some steed.

Wit. Wherewith, sweet Will? *Will.* Alas, by thine advice.

Wit. Whereto, good Will? *Will.* To win my wish with speed.

Wit. I know not how. *Will.* O Lord, that Will were wise !

Wit. Wouldst thou be wise? *Will.* Full fain. *Wit.* Then come from school.[1]

Take this of Wit : Love learns to play the fool.

[1] The words " Then come from school'" are given to *Will* in old ed.

THE SONG OF CARE.

COME, all the world, submit yourselves to Care,
    And him acknowledge for your chiefest king ;
With whom no king or keisar may compare,
    Who bears so great a sway in everything :
At home, abroad, in peace and eke in war,
Care chiefly stands to either make or mar.

The court he keeps is in a wise conceit,
    His house a head where reason rules the wit ;
His seat the heart that hateth all deceit,
    His bed the brain that feels no frantic fit,
His diet is the cates of sweet content :
Thus is his life in heavenly pleasure spent.

His kingdom is the whole world round about ;
    Sorrow his sword to such as do rebel ;
His counsel wisdom that decides each doubt ;
    His skill foresight, of things to come to tell ;
His chief delight is studies of device
To keep his subjects out of miseries.

O courteous king, O high and mighty Care,
    What shall I write in honour of thy name ?
But to the world by due desert declare
    Thy royal state and thy immortal fame.
Then so I end, as I at first begun,
Care is the King of kings when all is done.

From *The Strange Fortunes of Two Excellent Princes*, 1600.

A CONCEIT.

I WOULD thou wert not fair, or I were wise ;
·I would thou hadst no face or I no eyes ;
I would thou wert not wise, or I not fond ;
Or thou not free, or I not so in bond.

But thou art fair, and I cannot be wise :
Thy sunlike face hath blinded both mine eyes ;
Thou canst not be but wise, nor I but fond ;
Nor thou but free, nor I but still in bond.

Yet am I wise to think that thou art fair ;
Mine eyes their pureness in thy face repair ;
Nor am I fond, that do thy wisdom see ;
Nor yet in bond, because that thou art free.

Then in thy beauty only make me wise,
And in thy face the Graces guide thine eyes ;
And in thy wisdom only see me fond ;
And in thy freedom keep me still in bond.

So shalt thou still be fair and I be wise ;
Thy face shine still upon my cleared eyes ;
Thy wisdom only see how I am fond ;
Thy freedom only keep me still in bond.

So would I thou wert fair and I were wise ;
So would thou hadst thy face and I mine eyes ;
So would I thou wert wise, and I were fond ;
And thou wert free, and I were still in bond.

From *The Famous History of
Friar Bacon.*

PEGGY THE BROWN.

*To a Northern tune of " Cam'st thou not from New-
castle ? "*

TO couple is a custom,
   All things thereto agree :
Why should not I then love?
   Since love to all is free.

But I'll have one that's pretty,
   Her cheeks of scarlet dye,
For to breed my delight
   When that I lig her by.

Tho' virtue be a dowry,
   Yet I'll chuse money store :
If my love prove untrue,
   With that I can get more.

The fair is oft unconstant,
   The black is often proud,
I'll chuse a lovely brown :
   Come, fiddler, scrape thy crowd.

Come, fiddler, scrape thy crowd,
   For Peggy the brown is she
Must be my bride : God guide
   That Peggy and I agree.

AFTER THE WEDDING.[1]

A ND did not you hear of a mirth that befell
    The morrow after a wedding day,
At carrying a bride at home to dwell?
    And away to Twiver away, away!

The quintain was set and the garlands were made,
    'Tis a pity old custom should ever decay;
And woe be to him that was horsed on a jade,
    For he carried no credit away, away!

We met a consort of fiddle-de-dees,
    We set them a-cock-horse, and made them to play
The "Winning of Bullen" and "Upsie-frees;"[2]
    And away to Twiver away, away!

There was ne'er a lad in all the parish
    That would go to the plow that day
But on his fore-horse his wench he carries;
    And away to Twiver away, away!

The butler was quick and the ale he did tap,
    The maidens did make the chamber full gay;
The serving-men gave me a fuddling-cap,
    And I did carry it away, away.

[1] This ballad—with some slight textual variations—is given by Scott in the notes appended to *Waverley*.
[2] "The Winning of Bullen" and "Upsie Frees" are old dance tunes.

The smith of the town his liquor so took
  That he was persuaded the ground looked blue ;
And I dare boldly to swear on a book
  Such smiths as he there are but a few.

A posset was made, and the women did sip
  And simpering said they could eat no more ;
Full many a maid was laid on the lip :
  I'll say no more but so give o'er.

                            From *The History of George-a-*
                            Green, The Pindar of Wake-
                            field.

A LOVE-LETTER.

PROVE but as constant as th' art bold
  Thy suit shall never be controll'd ;
I am not to be bought or sold
  For wealth or treasure.

Let suitors fret and fathers rage,
Then keep me in an iron cage ;
Yet I myself to thee engage
  I'll use my pleasure.

Then be no longer discontent ;
I write no more than what is meant ;
With this my hand my heart is sent ;
  Be 't thine endeavour

To lay some plot how we may meet,
And lovingly each other greet
With amorous words and kisses sweet :
  Thine for ever.

From *The Second Part of the
Mirror of Knighthood. Now
Newly translated out of Span-
ish by R. P.*, 1583.

LOVE'S WILES.

WHO thinks himself at freedom most of all,
   And least esteems of Lady Venus' fire,
Let him not boast, for he may soonest fall,
   And quickly feel the fury of her ire :
Her blinded son such sudden shafts lets fly
That freest hearts are first enthralled thereby.

There is not one which may himself defend,
   By strength nor wit, from mighty Cupid's dart,
For that unseen he doth his arrows send
   And unperceived with pain doth pierce the heart,
Bereaving wholly all delight and joy,
Leaving behind distress and great annoy.

The wonted weal he into woe doth turn
   Of him that once despised hath his power :
His cold affection he doth cause to burn,
   And turns his sweet to most detested sour,
Triumphing most with terror to torment
The man that erst against his will was bent.

NO DELIGHT WITHOUT LOVE.

EXCEPT I love I cannot have delight,
It is a care that doth to life belong ;
For why [1] I hold that life in great despite
That hath not sour [2] mixt with sweet among.
And though the torments which I feel be strong,
Yet had I rather thus for to remain
Than laugh, and live, not feeling lover's pain.

HIS HEARTLESS MISTRESS.

THE drops of rain in time the marble pierce,
Submission makes the lion's heart relent ;
But, Love, thy cruel torments are so fierce,
That mischiefs new thou daily dost invent;
For she, whose sight my heart in sunder rent,
Regardeth neither of my faith nor grief,
Nor yet yields death, which is my sole relief.

[1] " For why " = because.
[2] A dissyllable (written "sower" in the early edition).

TO PASTORA.

FAIR Pastora, cease off delay,
　　With speed declare the certainty,
Whether thou wilt my love repay ;
　　If not, then know that I must die.

I wish for life that I might thee adore,
　　And largely show the love to thee I bear :
And if that thou offended seem therefore,
　　With speed by speech let it to me appear ;
Which done, then know that for a certainty,
Thy sentence given, I am prepared to die.

Thou well dost see, or plainly may'st perceive,
　　That long time since I had thee in regard :
Frame not thy lips thy lover to deceive,
　　With scoffs and scorns return not thy reward :
Which if thou do, I never will reply,
But meekly yield, as ready prest [1] to die.

---

[1] " Ready prest " = ready and eager.

From *The Sixth Book of the Mir-
ror of Knighthood, Being the
First Book of the Third Part.
. . . Translated by R.P.*, 1598.

THE PATIENT LOVER.

THOUGH I be scorned, yet will I not disdain,
   But bend my thoughts fair beauty to adore ;
What though she smile when I sigh and complain,
It is, I know, to try my faith the more :
      For she is fair, and fairness is regarded ;
      And I am firm, firm love will be rewarded.

Suppose I love and languish to my end,
And she my plaints, my sighs, my prayers despise :
O 'tis enough, when Fates for me do send,
If she vouchsafe to close my dying eyes ;
      Which if she do, and chance to drop a tear,
      From death to life that balm will me uprear.

LOVE'S MARTIAL KNIGHT.

IF I must (sweet Love) obey,
  Be pitiful to me, I pray,
And let me have my love's reward ;
With pity let her me regard,
And then thy quiver I will fill,
With arrows to content thy will.

  I for thee will[1] ever fight,
  My name shall be *Love's Martial Knight;*
  On my shield thee will I wear,
  Still thy colours will I bear ;
If thou help my heart distressed,
Thou shalt be [for] ever blessed.

  To my fair I will appeal
  That with me she gently deal.
  —Farewell, Hope ! Love will not yield :
  Yet I bear him on my shield !
The froward[2] boy is too too cross,
And delighteth in my loss.

[1] Old ed. " I for thee will I euer fight."
[2] Old ed. " toward."

From *The Eighth Book of the
Mirror of Knighthood : Being
the third of the third Part.
Englished out of the Spanish
Tongue,* 1599.

BLIND FORTUNE.

FORTUNE is blind, she looks on no man's need ;
  And deaf, she hearkens unto no man's call ;
And cruel, she respects not who doth bleed ;
And envious, she rejoiceth at one's fall.
No beauty can unmask her hoodwinked eyes,
No force can drive attention to her ears,
No grief make her dead-sleeping pity rise,
Nor is her envy thawed with virtue's tears.
She at adventures lets her favours fly,
Without proportion, without due regards :
The base unworthy now she mounts on high,
And fatteth dunghills with her best rewards.
Anon they tumble to their first estate,
And other on the tottering wheel are set :
Who never find repentance till too late,
And then they find it in sad sorrow's net.
Such Fortune is, and, oh, what hap have I
To serve a goddess lighter than the wind,
Constant in nothing but inconstancy,
As also envious, cruel, deaf and blind !
    Fortune is blind ; oh, what can me betide
    But blind mishap, that serve so blind a guide !

THE LOVER RECANTS HIS FORMER HERESY.

M Y heart will burst except it be discharged
　　Of his huge load, that doth oppress it so :
Streams stopped o'erflow the banks, if not enlarged,
And fire supprest doth much more fiercer grow :
　　Great woes ript up, but half the woe remains,
　　But pains concealed doth aggravate the pains.
Sing then, my soul, the story of my loss,
Form in sweet words the anguish of my mind :
Yet do not : singing ill becomes a cross,
Rather sigh out, how hard Love's yoke I find.
　　Love is a sickness, singing [is] a joy :
　　And pleasure is no packhorse for annoy.
But must I then, knowing Love a disease
That fills our souls with strange calamities,
Spite of my heart enforce myself to please,
And in mine own arms hug my miseries ?
　　And seeing still my state wax worse and worse,
　　Must I of force embrace and kiss my curse ?
I must, I must, Cupid hath sworn I must,
And 'tis in vain and bootless to resist :
Then be not, Love, oh, be not too unjust,
I yield me to thy rule, rule how thou list :
　　For my reclaimed rebellion shall bring forth
　　A treble duty to thy glorious worth.
Oh Love, sweet Love, oh high and heavenly Love,
The court of pleasure, paradise of rest !
Without whose circuit all things bitter prove,

Within whose centure [1] every wretch is blest :
  O grant me pardon, sacred deity,
  I do recant my former heresy !
And thou the dearest [2] idol of my thought,
Whom love I did, and do, and always will :
Oh pardon what my coy disdain hath wrought,
My coy disdain, the author of this ill :
  And for the pride that I have showed before,
  By Love I swear, I'll love thee ten times more.
Hast thou shed tears? those tears will I repay,
Ten tears for one, a hundred tears for ten.
Hath my proud rigour hunted thee astray?
I'll lose my life, or bring thee back agen :
  Each sigh I'll quittance with a thousand groans,
  And each complaint with a whole age of moans.
And when I find thee, as I find thee will,
Or lose myself in seeking what I love,
Then will I try with all true humble skill
Thy pity on my great offence to move :
  Till when, my griefs are more than tongue can tell,
  My days are nights, and every place is hell.

---

[1] Cincture.   [2] Old ed. "gearest."

LOVE'S A BEE, AND BEES HAVE STINGS.

ONCE I thought, but falsely thought
   Cupid all delight had brought,
And that love had been a treasure,
And a palace full of pleasure,
But alas ! too soon I prove,
Nothing is so sour as love ;
     That for sorrow my muse sings,
     Love's a bee, and bees have stings.

When I thought I had obtained
That dear solace, which if gained
Should have caused all joy to spring,
Viewed, I found it no such thing :
But instead of sweet desires,
Found a rose hemmed in with briars ;
     That for sorrow my muse sings,
     Love's a bee, and bees have stings.

Wonted pleasant life adieu,
Love hath changed thee for a new :
New indeed, and sour I prove it,
Yet I cannot choose but love it ;
And as if it were delight,
I pursue it day and night ;
     That with sorrow my muse sings,
     I love bees, though bees have stings.

POSIES.

L OVE resisted is a child ;
   Suffered, is a tiger wild.

The scourge of heaven and earth, hell, sea and land,
Is scourged and mastered by a human hand.

My heart's heart likes my heart, and I again
Like my heart's heart ; so both content remain.

Mars and Cupid differ far,
Love cannot agree with war ;
And till Mars and Love agree
Look not, Love, to conquer me.

If Fortune's hand be not a stop,
I will attain the highest top ;
The which if Fortune do deny,
Fortune is to blame, not I.

HIS MISTRESS' PERFECTIONS.

THAT brow which doth with fair all fairs excel,
　　Those eyes that shining lends the world his light,
That gracious mouth where all the Graces dwell,
That dimpled chin, the whetstone of delight,
　　　Those two rare mounts, of lilies and of roses,
　　　That in their swelling all content encloses :

That brow, eye, mouth, chin, and most dainty cheek,
Doth call, keep, hold, bind, and in gyves restrain
My heart, eye, ear, my thought, and judgment eke,
That no-wise force can free me thence again :
　　　Yet do I love my pleasing pain so well
　　　That 'bove all joys I prize my heavenly hell.

Let dunghill baseness and the earthy mind
His *summum bonum* place in what he list,
My soul, which strange divinity doth find
Within thy face's centure to consist,
　　　Will not consent that any other be
　　　My only good but only, only thee.

Thy brow shall be the dreadful snowy bar
Where I will daily for thy mercy plead ;
Thy shining eye my path-directing star ;
Thy mouth the laws, which I must keep, shall read ;
　　　Thy chin and cheek shall equal power bear,
　　　The first to cheer, the last to keep in fear.

And thou thyself, goddess of my desire,
In my heart's temple daily I'll adore;
No other deity will I admire,
No other power divine will I implore:
  Great goddess, keep me in thy favour-shine,
  My heart, eye, ear, my thought and judgment's thine.

FEAR NOT, FAINT HEART.

FEAR not, faint heart, time may prove
  A sovereign plaster for your love.
Such a faith so firmly grounded,
Such a love so kindly placed,
From a heart so deeply wounded,
From a person so well graced,
Needs must get the heart's desiring,
Though hope yet seem not to say it;
And though this time seem retiring,
Time hereafter may repay it.
    Fear not, faint heart, time may prove
    A sovereign plaster for your love.

CUPID'S SPORTING-PLACE.

WHATE'ER he is that would behold
　　Imperious Cupid's sporting-place,
Here to gaze let him be bold,
On this beauteous comely grace.

Here doth rarest beauty dwell,
On her brow doth Cupid sit;
This is she that doth excel,
Both for her beauty, love, and wit.

In her Cupid taketh rest,
Joy and bliss with her have end;
Who knoweth her is double blest,
Whose beauty day to night doth lend.

> From ANTHONY MUNDAY'S *Ze-
> lanto, the Fountain of Fame,*
> 1580.

THE SONG WHICH MISTRESS URSULA SUNG TO HER LUTE TO ZELANTO.

AS Love is cause of joy,
　　So Love procureth care ;
As Love doth end annoy,
　　So Love doth cause despair ;
But yet I oft heard say,
　　And wise men like did give,
That no one at this day
　　Without a Love can live.
And think you I will Love defy?
No, no, I love until I die.

Love knits the sacred knot,
　　Love heart and hand doth bind ;
Love will not shrink one jot,
　　But Love doth keep his kind ;
Love maketh friends of foes,
　　Love stays the commonwealth ;
Love doth exile all woes
　　That would impair our health :
Since Love doth men and monsters move,
What man so fond will love disprove?

Love keeps the happy peace,
　　Love doth all strife allay,
Love sendeth rich increase,
　　Love keepeth wars away ;
Love of itself is all,
　　Love hath no fellow-mate ;
Love causeth me and shall
　　Love those that love my state.
Then love will I until I die ;
And all fond love I will defie.

From *The Famous and Renowned History of Primaleon of Greece. Translated out of French and Italian into English by* A[NTHONY] M[UN-DAY], 1619.

THE HOPEFUL LOVER.

REASON and duty both commandeth me
To love and serve the sovereign of my life,
Whose virtues Time's eternal wonders be,
And sweet appeasers of heart-breaking strife.

Though day and night my sorrows do increase
Through my unworthiness to taste her grace,
Yet with my soul her heavenly looks make peace,
Whereby my thoughts some comfort do embrace.

If then ungentle Fate urge not constraint
To leave the place where my most comfort is,
One time or other she may hear my plaint
And with kind pity help what's now amiss.

Be not so cruel to thy servant then,
For thou shalt find him dutiful and true,
And to exceed common esteem of men
In loyalty ; and so, sweet soul, adieu !

KIND DISCONTENT.

H E that hath spent his time in silent moan,
   And ne'er saw merry minute in his life,
To sad conceit makes all his sorrows known,
Who (to forestall pleasure's ensuing strife)
      Tells him whole stories of sweet discontent,
      To add more vigour to his languishment.

In such a Heaven of inward happiness
My labouring thoughts are earnestly employed :
Hating the vulgar track of idleness
Wherein so many infant-wits have joyed,
      And finding that it doth such comfort bring,
      Kind Discontent, I hail thee as my king.

BEAUTY SAT BATHING.

B EAUTY sat bathing by a spring
   Where fairest shades did hide her ;
The winds blew calm, the birds did sing,
   The cool streams ran beside her.
My wanton thoughts enticed mine eye
   To see what was forbidden [1]
But better memory said Fie ;
   So vain desire was chidden.

[1] So *England's Helicon.*—The romance gives "hidden." (There are other trifling differences of reading.)

Into a slumber then I fell,
  And fond imagination
Seemed to see, but could not tell
  Her feature or her fashion :
But even as babes in dreams do smile
  And sometimes fall a-weeping,
So I awaked as wise that while
  As when I fell a-sleeping.

From *Piers Plainness' Seven
Years' Prenticeship.* By
H[ENRY]C[HETTLE]. 1595.

WILY CUPID.

TRUST not his wanton tears
    Lest they beguile ye ;
Trust not his childish sigh,
  He breatheth slily.
Trust not his touch,
  His feeling may defile ye ;
Trust nothing that he doth,
  The wag is wily.
If you suffer him to prate,
You will rue it over-late.
  Beware of him, for he is witty :
Quickly strive the boy to bind,
Fear him not for he is blind :
  If he get loose, he shows no pity.

From *Honour's Academy, or the Famous Pastoral of the Fair Shepherdess Julietta.* *Done into English by* R[OBERT] T[OFTE], *Gentleman,* 1610.

DEFIANCE TO LOVE.

LOVE, fare thou well, live will I now
Quiet amongst the greenwood bough.

Ill betide him that love seeks,
He shall live but with lean cheeks ;
He that fondly falls in love,
A slave still to grief shall prove.
    Love, fare thou well, live will I now
    Quiet amongst the greenwood bough.

What an ass and fool is he
That will serve and may go free ! [1]
In world's not a wench so fair
But I for my life more care.
    Love, fare thou well, &c.

I like not these dames so smooth
As would have men court and love ;
For as constant I them find
As the sea is or the wind.
    Love, fare thou well, &c.

[1] Old ed. " That may serue, and will goe free."

Once I loved one that was kind,
But she did what pleased her mind ;
Better 'tis ne'er to be born
Than live as another's scorn.
    Love, fare thou well, etc.

Then, Love, thee I do defy,
I hate thy bad dealing I ;
He is a fool that lives in pain,
A toy so small for to gain.
    Love, fare thou well, live will I now
    Quiet amongst the greenwood bough.

               From LADY MARY WROTH'S
               Urania, 1621.

LOVE, WHAT ART THOU ?

LOVE, what art thou ? a vain thought
  In our minds by fancy wrought :
Idle smiles did thee beget
While fond wishes made the net,
Which so many fools have caught.

Love, what art thou ? light and fair,
Fresh as morning, clear as th' air ;
But too soon thy evening change
Makes thy worth with coldness range :
Still thy joy is mixed with care.

Love, what art thou ? a sweet flower,
Once full-blown, dead in an hour ;
Dust in wind as staid remains
As thy pleasure or our gains,
If thy humour change to lour.

Love, what art thou? childish, vain,
Firm as bubbles made by rain ;
Wantonness thy greatest pride ;
These foul faults thy virtues hide :
But babes can no staidness gain.

Love, what art thou? causeless-curst.
Yet, alas, these not the worst ;
Much more of thee may be said.
But thy law I once obeyed ;
Therefore say no more at first.

WHO CAN BLAME ME IF I LOVE?

WHO can blame me if I love,
    Since Love before the world did move ?
When I loved not I despaired,
Scarce for handsomeness I cared ;
Since so much I am refined
As new framed of state and mind,
    Who can blame me if I love,
      Since Love before the world did move ?

Some in truth of Love beguiled
Have him blind and childish styled ;
But let none in these persist,
Since, so judging, judgment missed.
    Who can blame me ?

G

Love in chaos did appear ;
When nothing was yet he seemed clear
Nor when light could be descried,
To his crown a light was tied.
    Who can blame me ?

Love is truth and doth delight
Whereas honour shines most bright ;
Reason's self doth Love approve,
Which makes us ourselves to love.
    Who can blame me ?

Could I my past time begin,
I would not commit such sin
To live an hour and not to love,
Since Love makes us perfect prove.
    Who can blame me ?

From JAMES MABBE'S *Celestina*,
1631.

NOW SLEEP, AND TAKE THY REST.

NOW sleep, and take thy rest,
   Once grieved and pained wight,
Since she now loves thee best
   Who is thy heart's delight.
Let joy be thy soul's guest,
   And care be banished quite,
Since she hath thee expressed
   To be her favourite.

WAITING.

YOU birds whose warblings prove
    Aurora draweth near,
Go fly and tell my Love
    That I expect him here.
The night doth posting move,
    Yet comes he not again :
God grant some other love
    Do not my Love detain.

From HENRY FARLEY'S *St.
Paul's Church, her Bill for
the Parliament,* 1621.

A COMPLAINT.

TO see a strange outlandish fowl,
    A quaint baboon, an ape, an owl,
A dancing bear, a giant's bone,
A foolish engine move alone,
A morris dance, a puppet-play,
Mad Tom to sing a roundelay,
A woman dancing on a rope,
Bull-baiting also at the *Hope*,
A rimer's jests, a jugler's cheats,
A tumbler showing cunning feats,
Or players acting on the stage,—
There goes the bounty of our age :
        But unto any pious motion
        There's little coin and less devotion.

From RICHARD BRATHWAIT'S
The English Gentlewoman,
1631.

MOUNTING HYPERBOLES.[1]

SKIN more pure than Ida's snow,
  Whiter far than Moorish milk ;
Sweeter than Ambrosia too,
Softer than the Paphian silk,
Indian plumes or thistle-down,
Or May-blossoms newly-blown,
Is my mistress, rosy-pale,
Adding beauty to her veil.

[1] "An excellent piece of complimental stuff to catch a self-conceited one. Many you have of your sex who are too attentive auditors in the report of their own praises. Nothing can be attributed to them which they hold not properly due unto them. Which conceits many times so transports them as, Narcissus-like, they are taken with their own shadows, doting on nothing more than these encomiastic bladders of their desertless praises. Let me advise you, whose discretion should be far from giving light ear to such airy Tritons, to disrelish the oily compliments of these amorous sycophants."

From RICHARD BRATHWAIT'S
*The Arcadian Princess, or
The Triumph of Justice,* 1635.

*Argument. Themista reproves such, as being wedded
to their own opinion, will not incline to Reason,
but prefer a precipitate Will before a deliberate
Judgment.*

LIKE to a top, which runneth round
    And never winneth any ground ;
Or th' dying scion of a vine
That rather breaks than it will twine ;
Or th' sightless mole whose life is spent
Divided from her element ;
Or plants removed from Tagus' shore,
Who never bloom nor blossom more ;
Or dark Cimmerians who delight
In shady shroud of pitchy night ;
Or mopping apes who are possest
Their cubs are ever prettiest :
So he who makes his own opinion
To be his one and only minion,
Nor will incline in any season
To th' weight of proof or strength of reason,
But prefers Will precipitate
'Fore Judgment that's deliberate ;
He ne'er shall lodge within my roof
Till, rectified by due reproof,
He labour to reform this ill
By giving way to others' will.

From SAMUEL SHEPPARD'S *The Loves of Amandus and Sophronia*, 1650.

EPITHALAMIUM.

HEAVENLY fair Urania's son,
　Thou that dwell'st on Helicon,
Hymen, O thy brows impale,
To the bride the bridegroom hale.
Take thy saffron robe and come
With sweet-flowered marjoram ;
Yellow socks of woollen wear,
With a smiling look appear ;
Shrill Epithalamiums sing,
Let this day with pleasure spring ;
Nimbly dance ; the flaming tree　　*The Pine.*
Take in that fair hand of thine.
Let good auguries combine
For the pair that now are wed ;
Let their joys be nourished,
Like a myrtle, ever green,
Owned by the Cyprian queen,
Who fosters it with rosy dew,
Where her nymphs their sport pursue.
Leave th' Aonian cave behind
(Come, O come with willing mind !)
And the Thespian rocks, whence drill
Aganippe waters still.
Chastest virgins, you that are
Either for to make or mar,
Make the air with Hymen ring,
Hymen, Hymenaeus sing !

CHOSEN POEMS

OF

NICHOLAS BRETON.

From *A Flourish upon Fancy,*
1577.

A Gentleman being on a Christmas Eve in a very
solitary place, among very solemn company, where
was but small cheer, less mirth, and least music,
being very earnestly entreated to sing a Christmas
Carol, with much ado sung as followeth.

NOW Christmas draweth near, and most men make
　　good cheer,
　With heigh-ho, care away !
I, like a sickly mome, in drowsy dumps at home,
　Will naught but fast and pray.

Some sing and dance for life, some card and dice as
　　rife,
　Some use old Christmas games ;
But I, oh wretched wight ! in dole both day and night ·
　Must dwell, the world so frames.

In court what pretty toys, what fine and pleasant joys
　To pass the time away !
In country naught but care ; sour cheese-curds chiefest
　　fare ;
　For wine a bowl of whey.

For every dainty dish, of flesh or else of fish,
　And for your drink in court,
A dish of young fried frogs, sod houghs of mezled
　　hogs,
　A cup of small-tap wort.

And for each courtly sight, each show that may delight
　　The eye or else the mind ;
In country thorns and brakes, and many miry lakes,
　　Is all the good you find.

And for fine enteries, halls, chambers, galleries,
　　And lodgings many moe,
Here desert woods or plains, where no delight re-
　　　　mains,
　　To walk in to and fro.

In court, for to be short, for every pretty sport
　　That may the heart delight ;
In country many a grief, and small or no relief
　　To aid the wounded wight.

And in this desert place, I, wretch ! in woeful case,
　　This merry Christmas-time,
Content myself perforce to rest my careful corse :
　　And so I end my rime.

*In the latter end of Christmas the same gentleman was
　　likewise desired to sing; and, although against his
　　will, was content to sing as followeth.*

THE Christmas now is past, and I have kept my
　　　　fast
　　With prayer every day ;
And like a country clown, with nodding up and down,
　　Have passed the time away.

As for old Christmas games, or dancing with fine
    dames,
  Or shows, or pretty plays,
A solemn oath I swear, I came not where they were
  Not all these holy-days.

I did not sing one note, except it were by rote,
  Still buzzing like a bee,
To ease my heavy heart of some though little smart,
  For want of other glee.

And as for pleasant wine, there was no drink so fine
  For to be tasted here ;
Full simple was my fare, if that I should compare
  The same to Christmas cheer.

I saw no kind of sight that might my mind delight,
  Believe me, noble dame ;
But everything I saw did fret at woe my maw
  To think upon the same.

Upon some bushy balk full fain I was to walk
  In woods, from tree to tree,
For want of better room : but since my fatal doom
  Hath so appointed me,

I stood therewith content, till Christmas full was spent,
  In hope that God will send
A better yet next year, my heavy heart to cheer :
  And so I make an end.

From *The Arbour of Amorous Devices*, 1593-4.

A SWEET LULLABY.

COME, little babe, come, silly soul,
  Thy father's shame, thy mother's grief,
Born as I doubt to all our dole,
And to thyself unhappy chief :
    Sing lullaby and lap it warm,
    Poor soul that thinks no creature harm.

Thou little think'st and less dost know,
The cause of this thy mother's moan,
Thou want'st the wit to wail her woe,
And I myself am all alone :
    Why dost thou weep? why dost thou wail?
    And knowest not yet what thou dost ail.

Come, little wretch, ah silly heart,
Mine only joy, what can I more?
If there be any wrong thy smart,
That may the destinies implore :
    'Twas I, I say, against my will,
    I wail the time, but be thou still.

And dost thou smile? oh thy sweet face,
Would God Himself He might thee see,

No doubt thou would'st soon purchase grace,
I know right well, for thee and me :
    But come to mother, babe, and play,
    For father false is fled away.

Sweet boy, if it by fortune chance
Thy father home again to send,
If death do strike me with his lance,
Yet mayst thou me to him commend :
    If any ask thy mother's name,
    Tell how by love she purchased blame.

Then will his gentle heart soon yield :
I know him of a noble mind :
Although a lion in the field,
A lamb in town thou shalt him find :
    Ask blessing, babe, be not afraid,
    His sugared words hath me betrayed.

Then mayst thou joy and be right glad ;
Although in woe I seem to moan,
Thy father is no rascal lad,
A noble youth of blood and bone :
    His glancing looks, if he once smile,
    Right honest women may beguile.

Come little boy and rock a-sleep,
Sing lullaby and be thou still ;
I that can do naught else but weep,
Will sit by thee and wail my fill :
    God bless my babe, and lullaby,
    From this thy father's quality.

From   *Melancholic   Humours*,
1600.

SEE AND SAY NOTHING.

OH my thoughts, keep in your words,
   Lest their passage do repent ye ;
Knowing, fortune still affords
   Nothing, but may discontent ye.

If your saint be like the sun,
   Sit not ye in Phœbus' chair,
Lest, when once the horses run,
   Ye be Dedalus his heir.

If your labours well deserve,
   Let your silence only grace them ;
And in patience hope preserve,
   That no fortune can deface them.

If your friend do grow unkind,
   Grieve, but do not seem to show it :
For a patient heart shall find
   Comfort, when the soul shall know it.

If your trust be all betrayed,
   Try, but trust no more at all :
But in soul be not dismayed,
   Whatsoever do befall.

In yourselves yourselves inclose,
  Keep your secrecies unseen ;
Lest, when ye yourselves disclose,
  Ye had better never been.

And whatever be your state,.
  Do not languish over-long ;
Lest you find it, all too late,
  Sorrow be a deadly song.

And be comforted in this,
  If your passions be concealed,
Cross or comfort, bale or bliss,
  'Tis the best, is not revealed.

So, my dearest thoughts, adieu,
  Hark, whereto my soul doth call ye :
Be but secret, wise, and true,
  Fear no evil can befall ye.

A DOLEFUL PASSION.

OH, tired heart too full of sorrows,
In night-like days, despairing morrows ;
How canst thou think, so deeply grieved,
To hope to live to be relieved ?

Good fortune hath all grace forsworn thee,
And cruel care hath too much torn thee :
Unfaithful friends do all deceive thee ;
Acquaintance all unkindly leave thee.

Beauty out of her book doth blot thee,
And love hath utterly forgot thee :
Patience doth but to passion move thee,
While only honour lives to love thee.

Thine enemies all ill devise thee,
Thy friends but little good advise thee ;
And they who most do duty owe thee,
Do seem as though they do not know thee.

Thus pity weeps to look upon thee,
To see how thou art woe-begone-thee ;
And while these passions seek to spill thee,
Death but attends the hour to kill thee.

And since no thought is coming to thee,
That any way may comfort do thee,
Dispose thy thoughts as best may please thee,
That heaven of all thy hell may ease thee.

A FAREWELL TO LOVE.

FAREWELL, love and loving folly,
  All thy thoughts are too unholy :
Beauty strikes thee full of blindness,
And then kills thee with unkindness.

Farewell, wit and witty reason,
All betrayed by fancy's treason :
Love hath of all joy bereft thee,
And to sorrow only left thee.

Farewell, will and wilful fancy,
All in danger of a frenzy :
Love to beauty's bow hath won thee,
And together all undone thee.

Farewell, beauty, sorrow's agent ;
Farewell, sorrow, patience' pageant ;
Farewell, patience, passion's stayer ;
Farewell, passion, love's betrayer.

Sorrow's agent, patience' pageant,
Passion's stayer, love's betrayer,
Beauty, sorrow, patience, passion,—
Farewell, life of such a fashion.

Fashion, so good fashions spilling ;
Passion, so with passions killing ;
Patience, so with sorrow wounding ;—
Farewell, beauty, love's confounding.

H

A SOLEMN TOY.

IF that love had been a king,
    He would have commanded beauty :
But he is a silly thing,
    That hath sworn to do her duty.

If that love had been a god,
    He had then been full of grace :
But how grace and love are odd,
    'Tis too plain a piteous case.

No : love is an idle jest,
    That hath only made a word,
Like unto a cuckoo's nest,
    That hath never hatched a bird.

Then from nothing to conceive
    That may any substance be,
Yet so many doth deceive ;
    Lord of heaven, deliver me.

NICHOLAS BRETON.

A SMILE MISCONSTRUED.

BY your leave, a little while :
   Love hath got a beauty's smile
From on earth the fairest face—
But he may be much deceived,
Kindness may be misconceived,
   Laughing oft is in disgrace.—

Oh but he doth know her nature,
And to be that blessed creature,
   That doth answer love with kindness—
Tush, the phœnix is a fable ;
Phœbus' horses have no stable ;
   Love is often full of blindness.—

Oh but he doth hear her voice,
Which doth make his heart rejoice
   With the sweetness of her sound—
Simple hope may be abused.
Hears he not he is refused?
   Which may give his heart a wound.—

No : love can believe it never,
Beauty favours once and ever,
   Though proud envy play the elf:
Truth and patience have approved,
Love shall ever be beloved,
   If my mistress be herself.

A WAGGERY.

CHILDREN'S *Ahs* and women's *Ohs*,
    Do a wondrous grief disclose ;
Where a dug the t'one will still,
And the t'other but a will.

Then in God's name let them cry ;
While they cry, they will not die :
For but few that are so curst
As to cry until they burst.

Say, some children are untoward :
So some women are as froward :
Let them cry them, 'twill not kill them ;
There is time enough to still them.

But if pity will be pleased
To relieve the small diseased,
When the help is once applying,
They will quickly leave their crying.

Let the child then suck his fill,
Let the woman have her will ;
All will hush, was heard before ;
Ah and *Oh*, will cry no more.

AN ODD CONCEIT.

L OVELY kind, and kindly loving,
  Such a mind were worth the moving :
Truly fair, and fairly true,—
Where are all these, but in you ?

Wisely kind, and kindly wise ;
Blessed life, where such love lies !
Wise, and kind, and fair, and true,—
Lovely live all these in you.

Sweetly dear, and dearly sweet ;
Blessed, where these blessings meet !
Sweet, fair, wise, kind, blessed, true, —
Blessed be all these in you !

From *Pasquil's Madcap,* 1600.

AN INVECTIVE AGAINST THE WICKED OF THE WORLD.

THE wealthy rascal, be he ne'er so base,
  Filthy, ill-favoured, ugly to behold,
Mole-eye, plaice-mouth, dog's tooth, and camel's face,
Blind, dumb, and deaf, diseased, rotten, old,
Yet, if he have the coffers full of gold,
  He shall have reverence, curtsy, cap and knee,
  And worship, like a man of high degree.

He shall have ballads written in his praise,
Books dedicated to his patronage,
Wits working for his pleasure many ways,
Pedigrees sought to mend his parentage,
And linked perhaps in noble marriage ;
  He shall have all that this vile world can give him,
  That into pride, the devil's mouth, may drive him.

If he can speak, his words are oracles,
If he can see, his eyes are spectacles,
If he can hear, his ears are miracles,
If he can stand, his legs are pinnacles :
Thus in the rules of reason's obstacles,
  If he be but a beast in shape and nature,
  Yet, give him wealth, he is a goodly creature.

But, be a man of ne'er so good a mind,
As fine a shape as nature can devise ;
Virtuous and gracious, comely, wise, and kind,
Valiant, well given, full of good qualities,
And almost free from fancy's vanities :

Yet let him want this filthy worldly dross,
He shall be sent but to the Beggar's Cross.

The fool will scoff him, and the knave abuse him,
And every rascal in his kind disgrace him,
Acquaintance leave him, and his friends refuse him :
And every dog will from his door displace him.
Oh this vile world will seek so to deface him
    That, until death do come for to relieve him,
    He shall have nothing here but that may grieve him.

If he have pence to purchase pretty things,
She that doth loathe him will dissemble love ;
While the poor man his heart with sorrow wrings
To see how want doth women's love remove,
And make a jackdaw of a turtle-dove :
    If he be rich, worlds serve him for his pelf,
    If he be poor, he may go serve himself.

      *   *   *   *   *

Let but a dunce, a dizard, or a dolt
Get him a welted gown, a satin coat ;
Then though at random he do shoot his bolt,
By telling of an idle tale by rote,
Where wisdom finds not one good word to note :
    Yea, though he can but gruntle like a swine,
    Yet to the eight wise men he shall be nine.

But for a poor man, be he ne'er so wise,
Grounded in rules of wit and reason's grace,
And in his speeches never so precise,
To put no word out of discretion's place ;
Yet shall you see, in shutting up the case,
    A peasant sloven with the purse's sleight,
    Will hum and haw him quite out of conceit.

*   *   *   *   *

Take an odd vicar in a village-town,
That only prays for plenty and for peace ;
If he can get him but a threadbare gown,
And tithe a pig, and eat a goose in grease,
And set his hand unto his neighbour's lease,
    And bid the clerk on Sundays ring the bell,
    He is a churchman fits the parish well.

But, if he get a benefice of worth,
That may maintain good hospitality,
And in the pulpit bring a figure forth,
Of faith and works with a formality,
And tell a knave of an ill quality ;
    If with his preaching he can fill the purse,
    He is a good man, God send ne'er a worse.

But yet this simple idle-headed ass,
That scarce hath learned to spell the Hebrew names,
Sir John Lack-Latin with a face of brass,
Who all by rote his poor collations frames,
And after service falls to alehouse games,
    Howe'er his wit may give the fool the lurch,
    He is not fit to govern in the church.

While he that spends the labour of his youth,
But in the Book of the eternal bliss,
And can and will deliver but the truth,
In which the hope of highest comfort is,
That cannot lead the faithful soul amiss :
    However so his state of wealth decline,
    Deserves the title of the true divine.

From *The Longing of a Blessed Heart*, 1601.

WHAT IS LOVE?

MEN talk of love that know not what it is :
 For could we know what love may be indeed,
We would not have our minds so led amiss
With idle toys, that wanton humours feed ;
But in the rules of higher reason read
 What love may be, so from the world concealed,
 Yet all too plainly to the world revealed.

Some one doth fain love is a blinded god ;
His blindness him more half a devil shows :
For love with blindness never made abode,
Which all the power of wit and reason knows :
And from whose grace the ground of knowledge grows :
 But such blind eyes, that can no better see,
 Shall never live to come where love may be.

Some only think it only is a thought
Bred in the eye, and buzzeth in the brain,
And breaks the heart, until the mind be brought
To feed the senses with a sorry vein,
Till wits, once gone, come never home again :
 And then too late in mad conceit do prove,
 Fantastic wits are ever void of love.

Some think it is a babe of beauty's getting,
Nursed up by nature, and time's only breeding ;
A pretty work to set the wits a-whetting,

Upon a fancy of a humour's feeding :
Where reason finds but little sense in reading.
  No, no : I see, children must go to school ;
  Philosophy is not for every fool.

And some again think there is no such thing,
But in conceit a kind of coined jest ;
Which only doth of idle humours spring,
Like to a bird within a phœnix' nest,
Where never yet did any young one rest.
  But let such fools take heed of blasphemy,
  For love is high in his divinity.

But to be short, to learn to find him out,
'Tis not in beauty's eyes, nor babies' hearts ;
He must go beat another world about,
And seek for love but in those living parts
Of reason's light, that is the life of arts,
  That will perceive, though he can never see,
  The perfect essence whereof love may be.

It is too clear a brightness for man's eye ;
Too high a wisdom for his wits to find ;
Too deep a secret for his sense to try ;
And all too heavenly for his earthly mind ;
It is a grace of such a glorious kind
  As gives the soul a secret power to know it,
  But gives no heart nor spirit power to show it.

It is of heaven and earth the highest beauty,
The powerful hand of heaven's and earth's creation,
The due commander of all spirits' duty,

The Deity of angels' adoration,
The glorious substance of the soul's salvation :
  The light of truth that all perfection trieth,
  And life that gives the life that never dieth.

It is the height of good and hate of ill,
Triumph of truth, and falsehood's overthrow ;
The only worker of the highest will ;
And only knowledge that doth knowledge know ;
And only ground where it doth only grow :
  It is in sum the substance of all bliss,
  Without whose blessing all thing [*sic*] nothing is.

From *The Passionate Shepherd*, 1604.

WELCOME TO AGLAIA.

FLORA hath been all about,
    And hath brought her wardrobe out ;
With her fairest, sweetest flowers,
All to trim up all your bowers.
Bid the shepherds and their swains
See the beauty of their plains ;
And command them with their flocks
To do reverence on the rocks,
Where they may so happy be
As her shadow but to see.
Bid the birds in every bush,
Not a bird to be at hush ;
But to sit, chirp, and sing,
To the beauty of the spring.
Call the sylvan nymphs together,
Bid them bring their music hither ;

Trees, their barky silence break,
Crack yet though they cannot speak.
Bid the purest, whitest swan,
Of her feathers make her fan :
Let the hound the hare go chase,
Lambs and rabbits run at base :
Flies be dancing in the sun,
While the silk-worm's webs are spun :
Hang a fish on every hook,
As she goes along the brook :
So with all your sweetest powers
Entertain her in your bowers,
Where her ear may joy to hear
How ye make your sweetest quire :
And in all your sweetest vein,
Still Aglaia strike the strain.
But when she her walk doth turn,
Then begin as fast to mourn :
All your flowers and garlands wither,
Put up all your pipes together :
Never strike a pleasing strain
Till she come abroad again.

WORLDLY PARADISE.

WHO can live in heart so glad
As the merry country lad ?
Who upon a fair green balk
May at pleasure sit and walk,
And amid the azure skies,
See the morning sun arise ;
While he hears in every spring,
How the birds do chirp and sing :

Or, before the hounds in cry,
See the hare go stealing by :
Or, along the shallow brook,
Angling with a baited hook,
See the fishes leap and play
In a blessed sunny day :
Or to hear the partridge call,
Till she have her covey all :
Or to see the subtle fox,
How the villain plies the box ;
After feeding on his prey,
How he closely sneaks away,
Through the hedge and down the furrow
Till he gets into his burrow :
Then the bee to gather honey,
And the little black-haired coney,
On a bank for sunny place
With her forefeet wash her face :
Are not these, with thousands moe
Than the courts of kings do know,
The true pleasing spirits sights,
That may breed true love's delights ?
But with all this happiness,
To behold that shepherdess,
To whose eyes all shepherds yield
All the fairest of the field,
Fair Aglaia in whose face,
Lives the shepherds' highest grace :
In whose worthy wonder praise,
See what her true shepherd says.
She is neither proud nor fine,
But in spirit more divine :
She can neither lour nor leer,

But a sweeter smiling cheer :
She had never painted face,
But a sweeter smiling grace :
She can never love dissemble,
Truth doth so her thoughts assemble
That, where wisdom guides her will,
She is kind and constant still.
All in sum she is that creature,
Of that truest comfort's Nature,
That doth show (but in exceedings)
How their praises had their breedings.
Let then poets fain their pleasure,
In their fictions of love's treasure :
Proud high spirits seek their graces,
In their idol painted faces :
My love's spirit's lowliness,
In affection's humbleness,
Under heav'n no happiness
Seeks but in this shepherdess.
For whose sake I say and swear,
By the passions that I bear,
Had I got a kingly grace,
I would leave my kingly place
And in heart be truly glad ˙
To become a country lad ;
Hard to lie, and go full bare,
And to feed on hungry fare :
So I might but live to be,
Where I might but sit to see,
Once a day, or all day long,
The sweet subject of my song :
In Aglaia's only eyes
All my worldly paradise.

A SOLEMN LONG ENDURING PASSION.

I HAVE neither plums nor cherries,
  Nuts, nor apples, nor strawberries ;
Pins nor laces, points nor gloves,
Nor a pair of painted doves :
Shuttlecock nor trundle-ball,
To present thy love withal :
But a heart, as true and kind
As an honest faithful mind
Can devise for to invent,
To thy patience I present.
At thy fairest feet it lies :
Bless it with thy blessed eyes :
Take it up into thy hands,
At whose only grace it stands,
To be comforted for ever
Or to look for comfort never.
Oh it is a strange affect,
That my fancy doth effect !
I am caught and cannot start :
Wit and reason, eye and heart,
All are witnesses to me,
Love hath sworn me slave to thee.
Let me then be but thy slave,
And no further favour crave :
Send me forth to tend thy flock,
On the highest mountain rock ;
Or command me but to go
To the valley ground below :

All shall be alike to me,
Where it please thee I shall be.
Let my fate be what thou wilt,
Save my life, or see it spilt :
Keep [me] fasting on thy mountain,
Charge me not come near thy fountain :
In the storms and bitter blasts,
Where the sky all overcasts :
In the coldest frost and snow
That the earth did ever know,
Let me sit and bite my thumbs,
Where I see no comfort comes :
All the sorrows I can prove,
Cannot put me from my love.

THE DESCRIPTION AND PRAISE OF HIS FAIREST LOVE.

AT shearing time she shall command
The finest fleece of all my wool :
And if her pleasure but demand
The fattest from the lean to cull,
She shall be mistress of my store :
Let me alone to work for more.

My cloak shall lie upon the ground,
From wet and dust to keep her feet :
My pipe with his best measure's sound,
Shall welcome her with music sweet :
And in my scrip some cates at least
Shall bid her to a shepherd's feast.

My staff shall stay her in her walk,
My dog shall at her heels attend her:
And I will hold her with such talk
As I do hope shall not offend her:
My ewes shall bleat, my lambs shall play,
To show her all the sport they may.

Why, I will tell her twenty things,
That I have heard my mother tell;
Of plucking of the buzzard's wings,
For killing of her cockerel,
And hunting Reynard to his den
For frighting of her sitting hen:

How she would say, when she was young,
That lovers were ashamed to lie,
And truth was so on every tongue,
That love meant naught but honesty;
"And sirrah (quoth she then to me)
Let ever this thy lesson be:

Look when thou lovest, love but one,
And let her worthy be thy love:
Then love her in thy heart alone,
And let her in thy passions prove."

*   *   *   *   *

And I will tell her such fine tales,
As for the nonce I will devise:
Of lapwings and of nightingales,
And how the swallow feeds on flies;
And of the hare, the fox, the hound,
The pasture and the meadow ground.

I

And of the springs, and of the wood,
And of the forests and the deer,
And of the rivers and the floods,
And of the mirth and merry cheer,
And of the looks and of the glances
Of maids and young men in their dances :

Of clapping hands, and drawing gloves,
And of the tokens of love's truth,
And of the pretty turtle-doves,
That teach the billing tricks of youth.

TELL ME, TELL ME, PRETTY MUSE.

TELL me, tell me pretty muse,
   Canst thou neither will nor choose
But be busy with my brain,
Still to put my wits to pain?
Shall my heart within my breast
Never have an hour of rest?

Idle humour what doth ail thee?
Not a thought that can avail thee :
Be thou ne'er so woe-begone thee,
Beauty will not look upon thee ;
Fortune wholly hath forlorn thee ;
And for love, it hath forsworn thee.

But if virtue have procured thee,
And that honour have conjured thee

In affection's royalty
To discharge love's loyalty,
That the eye of truth may see,
Then do what thou wilt for me.

Work my wit unto thy will,
Keep thy hammers working still :
Use thine art in every thought,
With such temper to be wrought,
That Aglaia may approve
Virtue's skill in framing love.

But if any labour lack,
Or if either flaw or crack
Make the metal not so fine
That the work be not divine,
And well fit for honour's store,—
Never come at me no more.

SONNET.

PRETTY twinkling starry eyes,
How did nature first devise
Such a sparkling in your sight
As to give love such delight
As to make him, like a fly,
Play with looks until he die?

Sure ye were not made at first,
For such mischief to be cursed :

As to kill affection's care,
That doth only truth declare !
Where worth's wonders never wither,
Love and beauty live together.

Blessed eyes, then give your blessing,
That, in passion's best expressing,
Love that only lives to grace ye,
May not suffer pride deface ye,
But, in gentle thought's directions,
Show the praise of your perfections.

From *Choice, Chance and Change; or Conceits in their Colours,* 1606.

A FOUL IDLE SLUT.

SHE that is neither fair, nor rich, nor wise,
  And yet as proud as any peacock's tail ;
Mumps with her lips and winketh with her eyes,
And thinks the world of fools will never fail ;
Stands on her pantofles for lack of shoes,
And idly talks for want of better wit ;
Will have her will whatever so she lose,
And say her mind although she die for it ;
Is cousin-german to a jack-an-apes,
And sister to her mother's speckled sow ;
Kin to a codshead when he kindly gapes,
Aunt to an ass and cousin to a cow :
    What will be said of her, so fit for no man ?
    —"O fie upon her, 'twas a filthy woman !"

UPON A MERRY HONEST FELLOW THAT WAS OUT OF TUNE FOR HIS PURSE.

HE that was gotten in a Christmas night
 After a deal of mirth and merry cheer,
When Tom and Tib were in their true delight,
And he loved her, and she held him full dear ;
Brought up in plainness, truth, and honesty ;
Cannot away to hear of knavery ;
Lives with his neighbours in rare amity,
And cares not for this worldly bravery ;
Goes through the world with *yea* and *nay* and *so,*
And meddles with no matters of import :
When to his grave this honest man shall go,
What will the world of all his worth report ?
—" Here lies a man, like hives that have no honey,
An honest creature, but he had no money."

From *I Would, and Would Not,*
1614.

I WOULD, AND WOULD NOT.

I WOULD I had as much as might be had
 Of wealthy wishes, to the world's content :
That I might live all like a lusty lad,
 And scorn the world, and care not how it went :
But eat, and drink, and sleep, and sing, and play,
And so in pleasures, pass my time away.

And yet I would not : for, too wealthy then,
　　I should be troubled with a world of toys :
Kindred, companions, troops of serving-men ;
　　Fashion-devisers, fools, and girls and boys :
Fiddlers, and jesters, monkeys, apes, baboons,
Drunkards, and swaggerers, and such trouble-towns.

Besides I should forget to find the way,
　　That leads the soul to her eternal bliss ;
And then my state were at a woeful stay.
　　No, I would wish a better world than this,
And in afflictions here on earth to dwell
Rather than seek my heav'n on earth, and run to hell.

　　　*　　*　　*　　*　　*

I would I were an innocent, a fool,
　　That can do nothing else but laugh or cry :
And eat fat meat and never go to school ;
　　And be in love but with an apple-pie :
Wear a pied coat, a coxcomb, and a bell,
And think it did become me passing well.

And yet I would not : for then should I not
　　Discern the difference 'twixt the good and bad,
Nor how the gain of all the world is got,
　　Nor who are sober, wise, nor who are mad,
Nor in the truth of follies sense to see :
Who's the fool now ? there's no such fool as he ?

　　　*　　*　　*　　*　　*

I would I were a keeper of a park,
　　To walk with my bent cross-bow, and my hound,
To know my game, and closely in the dark
　　To lay a barren doe upon the ground,
And by my venison, more than by my fees,
To feed on better meat than bread and cheese.

And yet I would not : lest if I be spied,
   I might be turned quite out of my walk ;
And afterwards more punishment abide
   Than 'longs unto a little angry talk ;
And cause more mischief after all come to me
Than all the good the does did ever do me.

No, I would rather be an honest keeper,
   To walk my park, and look unto my pales ;
And not to play the sluggard and the sleeper,
   And hold my landlord up with idle tales ;
Take but my fees, be merry with my dame,
And so to gain and keep an honest name.

       *   *   *   *   *

I would I were a high astronomer,
   That I might make my walk among the stars :
And by my insight might foresee afar
   What were to come, and talk of peace and wars,
Of lives and deaths, and wonders to ensue,
Although perhaps but few do fall out true.

And yet I would not : for then do I doubt,
   With too much study I should grow stark mad :
When one conceit would put another out,
   While giddy brains beyond themselves would gad,
And, seeking for the man within the moon,
Mistake a morning for an afternoon.

No, I would rather learn no more to know
   Than of the times and seasons of the year :
What days the fairs are kept, and how to go
   From town to town, and every shire to shire ;[1]
That termers may not their day-notebooks slack,
And so to make an honest almanack.

---

[1] Pronounced " sheer " (and so written in the old edition).

*   *   *   *   *

I would I were a player, and could act
   As many parts as came upon a stage :
And in my brain could make a full compact,
   Of all that passeth betwixt youth and age ;
That I might have five shares in every play
And let them laugh that bear the bell away.

And yet I would not : for then do I fear,
   If I should gall some goose-cap with my speech,
That he would fret and fume, and chafe, and swear,
   As if some flea had bit him by the breech,
And in some passion or strange agony
Disturb both me and all the company.

I would I were a poet, and could write
   The passages of this paltry world in rime :
And talk of wars, and many a valiant fight,
   And how the captains did to honour climb :
Of wise, and fair, of gracious, virtuous, kind,
And of the bounty of a noble mind.

But speak but little of the life of love,
   Because it is a thing so hard to find ;
And touch but little at the turtle-dove,
   Seeing there are but few birds of that kind ;
And libel against lewd and wicked hearts,
That on the earth do play the devil's parts.

And yet I would not : for then would my brains
   Be with a world of toys intoxicate :
And I should fall upon a thousand veins,
   Of this and that, and well I know not what :
When some would say, that saw my frantic fits,
Surely the poet is beside his wits.

*   *   *   *   *

DEAD DELIGHT.[1]

AH, poor Conceit, Delight is dead !
    Thy pleasant days are done :
The shady dales must be his walk
    That cannot see the sun.

The world I now to witness call,
    The heavens my records be,
If ever I were false to Love
    Or Love were true to me.

I know it now, I knew it not,
    But all too late I rue it ;
I rue not that I knew it not,
    But that I ever knew it.

My care is not a fond conceit
    That breeds a feigned smart ;
My griefs do gripe me at the gall,
    And gnaw me at the heart.

My tears are not those feigned drops
    That fall from fancy's eyes,
But bitter streams of strange distress
    Wherein discomfort lies.

My sighs are not those heavy sighs
    That shews a sickly breath ;
My passions are the perfect signs,
    And very pains of death.

In sum, to make a doleful end,
    To see my death so nigh,
That sorrow bids me sing my last,
    And so my senses die.

[1] This poem was printed anonymously in "The Phœnix' Nest,"
1593. It is ascribed to Breton on early MS. authority. See Dr.
Grosart's edition of Breton, Part XXV., p. 20.

POEMS

FROM

CLEMENT ROBINSON'S "A HANDFUL OF PLEASANT
DELIGHTS," 1584; AND FROM "THE
PHŒNIX' NEST," 1593.

THE LOVER COMPARETH SOME SUBTLE SUITERS TO THE HUNTER.

To the tune of " The Painter."

WHENAS the hunter goeth out,
  With hounds in brace,
The hart to hunt and set about
  With wily trace,
He doth it more to see and view
Her wiliness (I tell you true),
  Her trips and skips, now here, now there,
  With squats and flats, which hath no peer ;

More than to win or get the game
  To bear away :
He is not greedy of the same ;
  Thus hunters say.
So some men hunt by hot desire
To Venus' dames, and do require
  By favour to have her, or else they will die ;
  They love her and prove her ; and wot ye why ?

Forsooth to see her subtleness
  And wily way,
When they (God knows) mean nothing less
  Than they do say :

For when they see they may her win,
They leave then where they did begin :
 They prate, and make the matter nice,
 And leave her in Fools' Paradise.

Wherefore, of such, good Lady, now
 Wisely beware,
Lest flinging fancies in their brow
 Do breed you care :
And at the first give them the check,
Lest they at last give you the geck [1]
 And scornfully disdaine ye then :
 In faith there are such kind of men.

But I am none of those indeed,
 Believe me now :
I am your man, if you be need ;
 I make a vow
To serve you without doubleness,
With fervent heart, my own mistress.
 Demand me, command me, what please ye and
  whan ;
 I will be still ready, as I am true man.

---

[1] "Give you the geck"—flout you.

A PROPER SONNET,

Intituled "*I smile to see how you devise.*"

To any pleasant Tune.

I SMILE to see how you devise
  New masking nets my eyes to blear;
Yourself you cannot so disguise
  But as you are you must appear.

Your privy winks at board I see,
  And how you set your roving mind :
Yourself you cannot hide from me ;
  Although I wink, I am not blind.

The secret sighs, and feigned cheer,
  That oft doth pain thy careful breast,
To me right plainly doth appear ;
  I see in whom thy heart doth rest.

And though thou mak'st a feigned vow
  That love no more thy heart should nip,
Yet think I know, as well as thou,
  The fickle helm doth guide the ship.

The salamander in the fire
  By course of kind doth bathe his limbs ;
The floating fish tak'th his desire
  In running streams whereas he swims.

So thou in change dost take delight ;
　　Full well I know thy slippery kind ;
In vain thou seem'st to dim my sight,
　　Thy rolling eyes bewray'th thy mind.

I see him smile that doth possess
　　Thy mind, which once I honoured most :
If he be wise, he may well guess
　　Thy love, soon won, will soon be lost.

And sith thou canst no man entice
　　That he should still love thee alone,
Thy beauty now hath lost her price ;
　　I see thy savoury scent is gone.

Therefore leave off thy wonted play ;
　　But as thou art thou wilt appear,
Unless thou canst devise a way
　　To dark the sun that shines so clear.

And keep thy friend that thou hast won ;
　　In truth to him thy love supply,
Lest he at length, as I have done,
　　Take off thy bells and let thee fly.

A PROPER SONG,

Intituled, "*Fain would I have a pretty thing to give unto my Lady.*"

To the tune of "Lusty Gallant."

FAIN would I have a pretty thing
　　To give unto my Lady:
I name no thing, nor I mean no thing,
　　But as pretty a thing as may be.

Twenty journeys would I make,
　　And twenty ways would hie me,
To make adventure for her sake,
　　To set some matter by me:
But I would fain have a pretty thing, etc.
I name no thing, nor I mean no thing, etc.

Some do long for pretty knacks,
　　And some for strange devices:
God send me that my lady lacks,
　　I care not what the price is.
Thus fain, etc.

Some go here, and some go there,
　　Where gazes[1] be not geason;[2]
And I go gaping everywhere,
　　But still come out of season.
Yet fain, etc.

I walk the town and tread the street,
　　In every corner seeking
The pretty thing I cannot meet
　　That's for my lady's liking.
Fain, etc.

[1] Shows to gaze at; gazingstocks.　　[2] Scarce, rare.

K

The mercers pull me, going by,
  The silk-wives say, "What lack ye?"
"The thing you have not," then say I :
  "Ye foolish knaves, go pack ye !"
But fain, etc.

It is not all the silk in Cheap,
  Nor all the golden treasure ;
Nor twenty bushels on a heap
  Can do my lady pleasure.
But fain, etc.

The gravers of the golden shows
  With jewels do beset me ;
The sempsters in the shops that sews,
  They do nothing but let me.
But fain, etc.

But were it in the wit of man
  By any means to make it,
I could for money buy it than,
  And say, " Fair Lady, take it."
Thus fain, etc.

O Lady, what a luck is this
  That my good willing misseth,
To find what pretty thing it is
  That my good lady wisheth.
Thus fain would I have had this pretty thing
  To give unto my lady :
I said no harm, nor I meant no harm,
  But as pretty a thing as may be.

A PROPER WOOING-SONG.

Intituled, "*Maid, will ye love me, yea or no?*"

*To the tune of "The Merchant's Daughter went over
the Field."*

MAID, will ye love me, yea or no?
Tell me the truth, and let me go.
It can be no less than a sinful deed,
    Trust me truly,
To linger a lover that looks to speed,
    In due time duly.

You maids, that think yourselves as fine
As Venus and all the Muses nine,
The Father himself when He first made man,
    Trust me truly,
Made you for his help, when the world began,
    In due time duly.

Then sith God's will was even so,
Why should you disdain your lover tho?[1]
But rather with a willing heart
    Love him truly :
For in so doing you do but your part ;
    Let reason rule ye.

Consider, Sweet, what sighs and sobs
Do nip my heart, with cruel throbs,

---

[1] "Tho"—then.

And all, my Dear, for love of you,
    Trust me truly :
But I hope that you will some mercy show,
    In due time duly.

If that you do my case well weigh,
And show some sign whereby I may
Have some good hope of your good grace,
    Trust me truly,
I count myself in a blessed case ;
    Let reason rule ye.

And for my part, whilst I do live,
To love you most faithfully, my hand I give ;
Forsaking all other for your sweet sake,
    Trust me truly :
In token whereof my troth I betake
    To yourself most duly.

And though for this time we must depart,
Yet keep you this ring, true-token of my heart :
Till time do serve we meet again,
    Let reason rule ye ;
When an answer of comfort I trust to obtain,
    In due time duly.

Now must I depart with sighing tears,
With sobbing heart and burning ears,
Pale in the face, and faint as I may,
    Trust me truly :
But I hope our next meeting a joyful day
    In due time duly.

By Thomas Lodge.

ACCURST BE LOVE !

ACCURST be Love, and those that trust his trains!
He tastes the fruit whilst others toil ;
He brings the lamp, we lend the oil ;
He sows distress, we yield him soil ;
He wageth war, we bide the foil.

Accurst be Love, and those that trust his trains !
He lays the trap, we seek the snare ;
He threat'neth death, we speak him fair ;
He coins deceits, we foster care ;
He favoureth pride, we count it rare.

Accurst be Love, and those that trust his trains !
He seemeth blind, yet wounds with art ;
He vows content, he pays with smart ;
He swears relief, yet kills the heart ;
He calls for truth, yet scorns desart.
Accurst be Love, and those that trust his trains !
Whose heaven is hell, whose perfect joys are pains.

By Thomas Lodge.

THE LOVER'S THEME.

FAIN to content, I bend myself to write,
    But what to write my mind can scarce conceive :
Your radiant eyes crave objects of delight,
My heart no glad impressions can receive :
      To write of grief is but a tedious thing,
      And woeful men of woe must needly [1] sing.

To write the truce, the wars, the strife, the peace,
That Love once wrought in my distempered heart,
Were but to cause my wonted woes increase,
And yield new life to my concealed smart :
      Who tempts the ear with tedious lines of grief,
      That waits for joy, complains without relief.

To write what pains supplanteth others' joy,
For-thy [2] is folly in the greatest wit :
Who feels may best decipher the annoy :
Who knows the grief but he that tasteth it ?
      Who writes of woe must needs be woe-begone,
      And writing feel, and feeling write of moan.

To write the temper of my last desire,
That likes me best, and appertains you most :
You are the Pharos whereto now retire

[1] Necessarily.   [2] Therefore.

My thoughts, long wand'ring in a foreign coast :
    In you they live, to other joys they die,
    And, living, draw their food from your fair eye.

Enforced by Love, and that effectual fire
That springs from you to quicken loyal hearts,
I write in part the prime of my desire,
My faith, my fear, that springs from your desarts :
    My faith, whose firmness never shunneth trial ;
    My fear, the dread and danger of denial.

To write in brief a legend in a line,
My heart hath vowed to draw his life from yours ;
My looks have made a sun of your sweet eyne,
My soul doth draw his essence from your powers :
    And what I am, in fortune or in love,
    All those have sworn to serve for your behove.

My senses seek their comforts from your sweet ;
My inward mind your outward fair admires ;
My hope lies prostrate at your pity's feet ;
My heart, looks, soul, sense, mind, and hope desires
    Belief and favour in your lovely sight :
    Else all will cease to live and pen to write.

By Thomas Lodge.

FOR PITY, PRETTY EYES, SURCEASE.

FOR pity, pretty eyes, surcease
　　To give me war ! and grant me peace.
Triumphant eyes, why bear you arms
Against a heart that thinks no harms ?
A heart already quite appalled,
A heart that yields and is enthralled ?
Kill rebels, proudly that resist ;
Not those that in true faith persist,
And conquered serve your deity.
Will you, alas ! command me die ?
Then die I yours, and death my cross ;
But unto you pertains the loss.

By Thomas Lodge.

LOVE'S WITCHERY.

MY bonny lass, thine eye,
　　　　So sly,
Hath made me sorrow so ;
Thy crimson cheeks, my dear,
　　　　So clear,
Have so much wrought my woe ;

Thy pleasing smiles and grace,
     Thy face,
Have ravished so my sprites,
That life is grown to nought
     Through thought
Of love, which me affrights.

For fancy's flames of fire
     Aspire
Unto such furious power
As, but the tears I shed
     Make dead
The brands would me devour,

I should consume to nought
     Through thought
Of thy fair shining eye,
Thy cheeks, thy pleasing smiles,
     The wiles
That forced my heart to die ;

Thy grace, thy face, the part
     Where art
Stands gazing still to see
The wondrous gifts and power,
     Each hour,
That hath bewitched me.

By Sir Walter Raleigh.[1]

THE EXCUSE.

CALLING to mind mine eye long went about
T'entice my heart to seek to leave my breast,
All in a rage I thought to pull it out,
By whose device I lived in such unrest :
    What could it say to purchase so my grace?
    —Forsooth, that it had seen my mistress' face.

Another time I likewise call to mind
My heart was he that all my woe had wrought ;
For he my breast, the fort of love, resigned,
When of such wars my fancy never thought :
    What could it say when I would have him slain?
    —But he was yours, and had forgot me clean.

At length when I perceived both eye and heart
Excused themselves as guiltless of mine ill,
I found myself was cause of all my smart,
And told myself, Myself now slay I will :
    But when I found myself to you was true,
    I loved myself because myself loved you.

---

[1] No author's name is given in "The Phœnix' Nest"; but the poem was quoted by Puttenham in 1589 as "a most excellent ditty, written by Sir Walter Raleigh."

NO MINUTE GOOD TO LOVE.

THE time when first I fell in love,
　　Which now I must lament ;
The year wherein I lost such time
　　To compass my content ;

The day wherein I saw too late
　　The follies of a lover ;
The hour wherein I found such loss
　　As care cannot recover ;

And last, the minute of mishap
　　Which makes me thus to plain ;
The doleful fruits of lovers' suits,
　　Which labour lose in vain :

Doth make me solemnly protest,
　　As I with pain do prove,
There is no time, year, day, nor hour,
　　Nor minute, good to love.

DISCONSOLATE.

THE gentle season of the year
  Hath made my blooming branch appear,
    And beautified the land with flowers ;
The air doth savour with delight,
The heavens do smile to see the sight,
    And yet mine eyes augments their showers.

The meads are mantled all with green,
The trembling leaves have clothed the treen,
    The birds with feathers new do sing ;
But I, poor soul ! when wrong doth wrack,
Attire myself in mourning black,
    Whose leaf doth fall amid his spring !

And, as you see the scarlet rose
In his sweet prime his buds disclose,
    Whose hue is with the sun revived ;
So, in the April of mine age,
My lively colours do assuage,
    Because my sunshine is deprived.

My heart, that wonted was of yore
Light as the winds abroad to soar,
    Amongst the buds, when beauty springs,
Now only hovers over you ;
As doth the bird that's taken new
    And mourns when all her neighbours sings.

When every man is bent to sport,
Then pensive I alone resort
    Into some solitary walk ;
As doth the doleful turtle-dove,
Who, having lost her faithful love,
    Sits mourning on some withered stalk.

There to myself I do recount
How far my woes my joys surmount,
    How Love requiteth me with hate ;
How all my pleasures end in pain,
How hate doth say my hope is vain,
    How fortune frowns upon my state.

And in this mood, charged with despair,
With vapoured sighs I dim the air,
    And to the gods make this request :—
That, by the ending of my life,
I may have truce with this strange strife,
    And bring my soul to better rest.

A COUNTER-LOVE.

Declare, O mind, from fond desires excluded,
That thou didst find erewhile, by love deluded.

AN eye, the plot whereon Love sets his gin ;
    Beauty, the trap wherein the heedless fall ;
A smile, the train that draws the simple in ;
Sweet words, the wily instrument of all :
    Entreaties, posts ; fair promises are charms ;
    Writing, the messenger that wooes our harms.

Mistress and servant, titles of mischance ;
Commandments done, the act of slavery ;
Their colours worn, a clownish cognisance ;
And double duty, petty drudgery :
    And when she twines and dallies with thy locks,
    Thy freedom then is brought into the stocks.

To touch her hand, her hand binds thy desire ;
To wear her ring, her ring is Nessus' gift ;
To feel her breast, her breast doth blow the fire ;
To see her bare, her bare a baleful drift ;
    To bait thine eyes thereon, is loss of sight ;
    To think of it, confounds thy senses quite.

Kisses, the keys to sweet consuming sin ;
Closings, Cleopatra's adders at thy breast ;
Feigned resistance then she will begin,
And yet unsatiable in all the rest :
    And when thou dost unto the act proceed,
    The bed doth groan and tremble at the deed.

Beauty, a silver dew that falls in May ;
Love is an egg-shell with that humour filled ;
Desire, a winged boy, coming that way,
Delights and dallies with it in the field :
    The fiery sun draws up the shell on high ;
    Beauty decays, Love dies, Desire doth fly.

Unharmed, give ear : that thing is hap'ly caught,
That cost some dear, if thou mayst ha't for naught.

THE LOVER'S HEART.

TO make a truce, sweet Mistress, with your eyes,
  How often have I proffered you my heart !
Which proffers, unesteemed, you despise,
As far too mean to equal your desart :
    Your mind, wherein all high perfections flow,
    Deigns not the thought of things that are so low.

To strive to alter his desires were vain,
Whose vowed heart affects no other place ;
The which since you despise, I do disdain
To count it mine, as erst before it was ;
    For that is mine which you alone allow,
    As I am yours and only live for you.

Now, if I him forsake and he not find
His wretched exile succoured by your eyes,
He cannot yield to serve another's mind,
Nor live alone ; for nature that denies :
    Then die he must, for other choice is none,—
    But live in you or me, or die alone.

Whose hapless death, when Fame abroad hath blown,
Blame and reproach procures unto us both ;
I, as unkind, forsaking so mine own ;
But you much more, from whom the rigour grow'th :
    And so much more will your dishonour be,
    By how much more it loved you than me.

Sweet lady, then the heart's misfortune rue,
Whose love and service evermore was true.

THE DESCRIPTION OF JEALOUSY.

A SEEING friend, yet enemy to rest ;
   A wrangling passion, yet a gladsome thought ;
A bad companion, yet a welcome guest ;
A knowledge wished, yet found too soon unsought :
    From heaven supposed, yet sure condemned to
        hell
    Is jealousy, and there forlorn doth dwell.

And thence doth send fond fear and false suspect
To haunt our thoughts, bewitched with mistrust ;
Which breeds in us the issue and effect
Both of conceits and actions far unjust ;
    The grief, the shame, the smart whereof doth
        prove
    That jealousy's both death and hell to love.

For what but hell moves in the jealous heart,
Where restless fear works out all wanton joys,
Which doth both quench and kill the loving part,
And cloys the mind with worse than known annoys,
    Whose pressure far exceeds hell's deep extremes ?
    Such life leads Love, entangled with misdeems.

LOVE HATH EYES BY NIGHT.

O NIGHT, O jealous Night, repugnant to my
measures ![1]
O Night so long desired, yet cross to my content !
There's none but only thou that can perform my
pleasures,
Yet none but only thou that hindereth my intent.

Thy beams, thy spiteful beams, thy lamps that burn too
brightly,
Discover all my trains and naked lay my drifts,
That night by night I hope, yet fail my purpose
nightly ;
Thy envious glaring gleam defeateth so my shifts.

Sweet Night, withold thy beams, withold them till
tomorrow !
Whose joy's in lack so long a hell of torment breeds.
Sweet Night, sweet gentle Night, do not prolong my
sorrow :
Desire is guide to me, and Love no lodestar needs.

Let sailors gaze on Stars, and Moon so freshly shining ;
Let them that miss the way be guided by the light ;

---

[1] Old ed. "pleasures."

L

I know my Lady's bower, there needs no more
    divining ;
  Affection sees in dark, and Love hath eyes by
    night.

Dame Cynthia, couch awhile ! hold in thy horns for
    shining,
  And glad not lowring Night with thy too glorious
    rays ;
But be she dim and dark, tempestuous and repining,
  That in her spite my sport may work thy endless
    praise.

And when my will is wrought, then, Cynthia, shine,
    good lady,
  All other nights and days in honour of that night,
That happy heavenly night, that night so dark and
    shady,
  Wherein my Love had eyes that lighted my delight !

NOTES.

NOTES.

Page xvii. *R. P.* There was a Robert Parry who in 1595 published a romance "Moderatus, or the Adventures of the Black Knight." I suspect that this person was the "R. P." who is responsible for a portion of the "Mirror of Knighthood" (though there is another claimant to the initials—Richard Parre).

There is plenty of verse in "Moderatus," but it is of poor quality. As the romance is of the highest rarity, I will find room here for one of the poems, a warning to incautious maids :—

> "What fancies foul doth silly maids entice
> To like and love the false and flattering wight !
> What viper would the selfsame thing despise
> Which erst he sought with all his force and might !
>   But fond I was ; and fickle his desire,
>   Like bavin's blaze that soon was set on fire.

> Such fire it was that wrought my deep annoy ;
> Such fool I was that credulous would prove,
> And trust repose in him that did but toy
> And, full of lust, would counterfeit some love :
>   Lo, to my care, with grief of heart I find
>   His flattering words, which were but blasts of wind.

> What cockatrice so pleasant once could smile,
> And cover fraud with such a glorious bait !

Who would have thought such beauty covered guile ;
But fowlers still, their snares being laid, do wait
    And counterfeit, the silly birds to trap :
    So did this wretch, the more is my ill-hap."

Page xxvi. "A Post with a Packet of Mad Letters."
The first letter that I will quote is "A Letter to his
Mistris desiring Marriage." It is a frank, straight-
forward proposal, couched in language that precludes
all possibility of future misunderstanding :—

"Courteous Mistris *Amee*, the only joy of my heart,
I thought it fitting to declare my minde in writing to
you : long time haue I rested your true and constant
loue, hoping to finde the like true affection from you :
I write not in any dissembling sort, my tongue doth
declare my heart, assuring you that I doe not regard
any portion, but your hearty loue to remaine firme to
me. I would be glad to know when you would appoint
the day of our marriage, if it stand so to your liking :
deare *Amee*, take some pitty on him that loueth you so
well : you know that I haue beene profferd good mens
daughters in mariage, but I could neuer fancy any so
well as your selfe. I desire to know the fulnesse of your
affection, whether it doth equall mine or no, and upon
the receit of your answer, you shall see me shortly after :
(though I receiue you in your smocke,) I haue sufficient
meanes to prouide for you and me both. I haue sent
you a ring in token of loue, which I pray you accept of.
I omit all eloquence, not doubting but you will consider
my feruent zeale which cannot be expressed with words.
Thus requesting your answer, I commit you to God,
resting

Your assured loving friend till death, H. K."

The four following letters relate to a love-quarrel and reconciliation ;—

A Letter to laugh at after the old fashion of love to a Maid.

"After my hearty commendations, trusting in God that you are in good health as I was at the writing hereof, with my Father, my Mother, my Brothers and Sisters, and all my good friends, (thanks be to God). The cause of my writing to you at this time, is, that *Margery*, I doe heare since my comming from *Wakefield*, when you know what talke wee had together at the signe of the blue Cuckoe, and how you did giue me your hand, and sweare that you would not forsake me for all the world : and how you made me buy a Ring and a Heart, that cost me eighteéne pence, which I left with you, and you gaue me a Napkin to weare in my Hat, I thanke you, which I will weare to my dying day. And I maruell if it be true as I heare, that you haue altered your mind, & are made sure to my neighbour *Hoglins* younger Son. Truly *Margery* you do not well in so doing, and God will plague you for it : and I hope I shal liue, and if I neuer haue you : for there are more maids thē *Maulkin*, and I count myselfe worth the whistling after. And therefore praying you to write me your answer by this bearer my friend, touching the truth of all how the matter stands with you, I commit you to God, From *Callowgreene*,

Your true love, R. P."

Her Answer.

"Truely *Roger*, I did not looke for such a Letter from your hands : I would you should know I scorne it :

Haue I gotten my Fathers, and Mothers ill will for you, to bee so vsed at your hands? I perceiue, and if you be so jealous already, you would bee somewhat another day. I am glad I finde you, that you can beleéue any thing of me : but it is no matter, I care not : send me my Napkin, and you shall haue your Ring and your Heart, for I can haue enow if I neuer sée you more : for there are more Batchelors then *Roger*, and my penny is as good siluer as yours, and therefore seeing you are so lustie, euen put vp your pipes for I will haue no more to doe with you : And so vnsaying al that euer hath beene said betwixt vs, make your choise where you list, I know where to be beloued, and so I end, from *Wakefield*,

M. R."

Roger to Margerie his Sweet-heart.

"*Margerie*, I haue receiued your snappish Letter, whereby I sée you are more angry, then I thought you would haue beéne for a mis-word or two, but I hope to mend what is amisse : for I sée I was too blame : for now I find the knauery of the world, I will looke a little better to my selfe : for it was your Cousins doing to de-uise lies, to set you and me out, but if you will be ruled by me, wée will méet with them well enough : vpon Friday I wil méet you at the market : where we will haue a Cake and a Pot, at the Pickerill and Spurre, there we will strike vp a bargaine, that will not be broken in hast : and so sorry with all my heart that I haue done as I haue done : sending thée twenty kisses by my sister *Parnell*, and this bowed Groat for a Loue-token, I rest,

Yours from all the world R. P."

Her Answer.

"Oh *Roger*, the world is well amended: I thought you were misused, to write to me as you did : but friends are nere so farre out, but they may be as far in againe : and therefore since it was against your will, I forgiue you with all my heart : & let my cousin doe his worst, Ile not goe from my word : on Friday Ile méet you at ten of the clock, and bring a péece of bacon in my pocket, to relish a cup of Ale, when it shall goe hard, if all hit right, but some body shall wipe their nose for their knauery, and so *Roger*, hoping that you will no more abuse me as you haue done, to beléeue lies and tales of me, till you know the truth, treading all vnkind-nesse vnder foot, I rest, with all my heart, as I was and will be euer.   *Yours as you know, M. R.*"

I now quote a letter from a gentleman detained in London on legal business to his wife in the country ; with the wife's answer :—

To a wife in the Country.

" Good Wife, in all kindnesse I commit me to thy self, assuring thée that I thinke it long till I haue dispatched my businesse, and am at home againe : But I hope of good successe in my suite, for my Counsell doth war-rant my case cleere : Vpon Friday next I shall haue triall, which I doubt not will goe on my side : if it doe not, my thought is taken, for I thanke God I can liue without it, though I would be loath to lose it.   My health, I thanke God, I haue well, and pray for the same to thée and thine.   I pray you send me vp twenty pounds by this Bearer, with al spéed, and within fiue daies after the dispatch of my businesse, expect my

comming downe : in the meane time kisse my little
Babes for mée, to whom with thy selfe, I send my
hearts hoping commendations, and so in haste I commit thée to the Almightie.

London   Your very loving Husband, R. T."

Her Answer.

" Swéet-heart, your Messengers haste makes mee
briefer than other wise I would be : the good dispatch
of your businesse I hope, and heartily pray for : your
health I am glad of, and your returne cannot be so
soone as wished for.   Your money I haue sent by this
Bearer.   Your little ones with my selfe would be glad
to see you, who doe not a little misse you for diuers
causes too tedious at this time to trouble you withall :
But in any wise remember your Girles Cawle, and your
Boyes Hat, which will not be a little welcome.   But
good Husband, make one end or another with it this
Tearme, lest delaies and demurres, make you to spend
more in it then it is worth : But you know what to doe
better than I can aduise you : and therefore leauing it
to your discretion, to doe what shall best please you, I
commit you to God, and rest, in haste.

Chaulkley.   Your very loving Wife, M. T."

I will end with two business letters, touching the
purchase of some property :—

A Letter to a friend for dispatch of businesse.

" I am bold to intreat your kindnesse, to stead mée
in what you may touching the purchase of the Mills
and Hop-gardens, for which if your neighbour will take

mine offer, I am for him, or else I must otherwise determine of my money that I haue reserued onely for that vse. I am offered great penny-worths in diuers places : but the ayre pleaseth me well about that house, and the trouts in the little brookes haue made me haue a great mind to dwell thereabouts : if therefore you can bring him to my price, I will be beholding to you : if not, let me know his mind, and I am satisfied : for to tel you the troth, I would haue it though it cost me more then it is worth, and so intreating you to do mée what good you can herein for which you shall not find me vnthankfull, I rest,

Your loving friend, A. W."

The Answer.

" I receiued your Letter, dated the xiii of this month, whereby I vnderstand your mind touching the lease of the two Milles and Hopp-gardens : but I cannot bring it to passe one penny vnder the Summe, whervpon he tels me you were in a manner agréed :·the man is hard but very honest : and the land good, and lieth finely to the house : the Soyle is healthfull : and there is good store of Springs : besides the Riuer is not farre off, whereby you may haue carriage wéekley from the City vpon a small reckoning : but vse your discretion, the price you know, and mée you may command, but time would not be deferred, for there are many about it : and therefore leauing to your discretion, either to take it, or refuse it, with assurance of my helpe to the vtmost of my power, either in this or what else may pleasure you, I alwaies rest,

Yours as you know, T. D."

Page xxvi. *The Miseries of Mavillia.* Mavillia was certainly an ill-starred lady. When she was in her fifth year the town in which she resided was sacked, and her father and mother were brutally murdered. A poor laundress in the train of the victorious army took charge of the young Mavillia, but treated her with scant kindness. When her parents were alive the little creature had been universally petted. Her father would take her by the chin and call her his good girl, his sweet mouse, and dad's bird. He had always an apple or a pear ready for her. The neighbours, too, made much of her, and every pretty child was glad to play with her. But now the case was altered. If she cried for a little drink, or some bread and butter, or asked to be put to bed, the laundress was after her with a birchen rod. Then if she happened to be playing with the cat or the dog, or making a doll out of some old rags, up would come the laundress, slap her in the face, toss her by the shoulders, and set her to study her Christ-cross row—the alphabet of the old primers. The child was an apt pupil, and soon learned to read any place in the bible, so that then her protectress took some delight in her and used her more kindly. Her needlework gave her some distress at first, and she got many a clout on the ear from the old dame ; but by perseverance she became skilful with her needle. At length the town was recaptured by her own countrymen, and she was treated with every consideration by the captain. He arranged that she should be sent to her uncle's house far away, and appointed certain gentlemen (together with his own page) to conduct her. As she and her escort were passing through a wood they were attacked by brigands. The fight was so fierce

that all were killed except Mavillia and the page. The
two trudged along—all the horses had been killed—
through that day and through the night and the next
morning. They were very hungry ; the poor page had
got his pistol ready in case he should sight a pigeon,
but no pigeon could he see. By good luck, however,
a cow wandered their way ; they uttered a hasty
prayer that she would stand still " till they had gotten
of her milk to comfort themselves withal," and then
Mavillia took off her hat and milked the cow into it,
the creature making no resistance. They each had a
good draught and kept some in the hat for the mor-
row. But a sad accident befell on the next night. The
page, lying down on a bank to take a snatch of rest
(for he was quite worn out), leaned inadvertently on
his dag or pistol, which was under his girdle ; where-
upon the pistol discharged a bullet into his right hip.
Mavillia was deeply distressed, but the page bore up
right manfully. " Mistress," quoth he, " the hurt
grieves me not so much as to think how I am hindered
from my hearty desire to show mine humble duty in
conducting you to your uncle's house. But since God
hath laid His punishment upon me, I beseech Him to
grant me His grace to take it patiently : alas ! I
think I am the most unhappy villain in the world.
But, mistress, this is the world ; a man that hath
travelled many countries and passed great perils, being
tossed in many tempests among the boiling billows of
sore seas, in the end comes home and perhaps walking
but through his own ground, his foot slips off a bridge
and [he] is drowned in a ditch." Mavillia tends the
page with devoted care, and having a knowledge of
simples succeeds in procuring him some relief from

his pain. While they are speculating as to how they shall get their next meal the page observes a fox carrying off a lamb. Mavillia runs after the fox and frightens him with a loud cry, so that he drops the lamb, which they proceed to dress and cook. The lamb lasted them for some days until the page was strong enough to start again on the journey, leaning one hand on Mavillia's shoulder and resting on a staff with the other. They passed through a great forest and came to a high hill. When they had gone over the hill, they found on the other side a huge boar waiting, who rushed with open mouth at the poor page. The page shot him through the head, but not before he had been sorely wounded by the boar in the leg. Mavillia bound up the hurt; then on they went again, and presently came to a cottage belonging to a poor shepherd. The shepherd's wife (a crabbed old woman) and her daughter were within. After some to-do the wanderers are admitted, and the page is put to bed. But he is past all help, and dies the same night. On his death-bed he hands a purse full of gold to the old woman for her own use (for he had taken all the money that he could find on his dead friends and their assailants) and lays injunctions that Mavillia is to want for nothing; and he gives another purse of gold that is to be kept until Mavillia demands it. The next morning the old dame begins betimes to give proofs of her churlish condition. She insists that Mavillia is to put off her gentlewoman's apparel and wear coarse clothing if she wants to see the page buried. After the funeral Mavillia's troubles start afresh. The old dame sets her to hemming hempen stuff with a great coarse needle. As for the money left by the page,

the shepherd spends it in purchasing a piece of land
and a fair house. Mavillia has to card, and knit,
and brew, and bake, weed the garden, feed the hogs,
scour pots, turn the spit, sweep the house out; and to
help her there was but one other maid who was such
an idle baggage that she would do nothing but sleep.
When the shepherd moved into his fair house other
servants were taken, and Mavillia was set to attend on
the old woman's daughter, "the most ill-favoured and
untoward urchin that ever was born." "This baggage
must I go teach her book, and forsooth touch her I
must not, but 'Good mistress, look on your book.
Yea, that is a fair gentlewoman,' when she said never
a word, but I was fain to speak for her. If I com-
plained of her then 'O you think much of your pains;
would you have her read as well as you the first day?
Go, come not to me with such twittle twattle': then
[would she] go to the girl, 'Doth she say thou wilt not
learn? Marry, she lies. Hold here, wilt thou have a
plum or an apple? Yea, marry it is a good girl': then
was I glad to get apples and pears and such gear to
bring her to the book. And then the apish elf for my
heart would not say a word, so that I could not for my
life but give her a little slap on the shoulders; and if I
did but even touch her the monkey would set out the
throat and cry so vengeously that to it must the
mother come, and then 'How now, girl? tell me, doth
she beat thee? Minion, you were best not touch her,
see you; the wench would learn well enough, an you
were willing to teach her: well, ye were best use her
gently lest ye fare the worse for it'; and so away she
goes. Now would I sit weeping for grief that the
squall would learn no faster; and if the hilding had

got out of my sight that she had run paddling about, and by chance spotted any of her clothes, or taken a fall (and yet it was old enough, being betwixt seven and eight years of age, to go alone), yet, as I say, if aught was amiss with her, I was checked, snibbed, called proud minx, rated like a dog, and now and then beaten so extremely if the old crone were in an angry mood, as she was seldom little better." The only grain of comfort for Mavillia was that the old shepherd took her part. When his wife was laying on her with a faggot-stick he would often interfere. Sometimes, when his wife was out of the way, he would produce from his pocket pieces of white bread and roast meat ; and from time to time he would give her a piece of gold and bid her lay it up for her marriage. After three or four years the old dame was seized with the gout in her toes, fingers, knees and almost all her joints ; and so violently was she racked that Mavillia —in spite of all the ill-treatment she had received— was frequently moved to tears. At length she died of the gout, covetous to the last, and leaving not a groat to Mavillia who had tended her so patiently. Shortly afterwards the shepherd fell ill and Mavillia had to nurse him. He grew worse and worse, and feeling that his end was near, he called one or two trusted neighbours, and gave special injunctions that Mavillia was to receive at his death five hundred pounds. The knavish executors determined to defraud poor Mavillia. Finding in a chest the gold pieces which the shepherd had given her and which she had carefully hoarded, they accused her of having stolen the money. The constable was summoned and she was carried before the justice, a vicious little maidservant giving evidence against her, and sent to gaol to await her trial. She passed a miserable time in gaol, shocked by the vile behaviour of her fellow-prisoners. At the trial her former pupil, the shepherd's daughter,—who has meanwhile been married, and from being a rude chit has become a graceful young lady—gives evidence in her favour. The maid who had brought the charge, repents of her villainy and confesses the truth. Mavillia receives her five hundred pounds from the executors, and goes on a visit to the house of her former pupil. Divers gentlemen now became suitors to her. Among them was an "old doting lover, a rich chuff in the country, who having lately buried his old Jone" now made up to Mavillia. She hated the sight of him, and the stubble of his rough old shaven beard used to vex her extremely. She could not away with the stale jests of the old dizard; he was as deaf as a door, and croop-shouldered; but he went bravely,—he had a fair chain about his neck, a brooch in his hat, and on his finger a seal ring with an ounce of gold in it at least. Mavillia's affections were fixed on a very different sort of person,—a young gentleman of grace and refinement, who was her devoted admirer. To escape from the importunity of her ancient suitor she agreed to marry the young man privately. But the old fellow got tidings of the matter, and on the marriage-day turned up at the church door, and in threatening words swore to be revenged. He wreaked his vengeance in a most horrible manner. She was walking abroad some time afterwards with her husband to see after some sheep that belonged to them, when a couple of merciless knaves (hired for the purpose) ran up with drawn swords, the old ruffian following on horseback. The

M

bravoes seized her husband by the shoulders and shook him like a dog. Mavillia implored for mercy for her husband with all earnestness and eloquence. The scoundrel seemed to relent and said " Well then, come hither, let me have a kiss for all the love I have borne thee, and so I will bid thee farewell." With tears of gratitude in her eyes Mavillia went forward to be kissed, and the villain—*horresco referens*—bit off her nose. Poor Mavillia! She bitterly resented the outrage, and implored Heaven to take vengeance on the wretch who had wronged her :—" O rascal, begotten in an ill hour, born to mischief, brought up in villainy and continuing in the same, Heaven will plague thee, and those teeth that tare my harmless face will the devil tear out with a hot firehook!" Her husband afterwards succeeded in killing the old scoundrel. She concludes her story at the point where her husband comes home wounded by some friends of the wretch he had killed ; she drops her pen in order to attend to his comfort.

Page xxvii. " The Eel and the Magpie."—So far as the magpie is concerned, this is an old story re-told ; but I can say nothing about the eel. I keep the old spelling, for it heightens the quaintness of the tale :—

"A neighbour of mine, in good case to liue, though not verie wealthie, and yet such a one as with his formality on a Hollidaie at Church would haue bene taken for the Hedborough of the Parish ; this honest substantiall man, drawing one daie a Mill-poole, among other fish, lighted on a verie great Eele : which, hauing got on lande, hee brought into his house, and put it with small Eeles into a Cesterne, where, feeding of it euery Morning and Euening, hee made (as it

were) an Idoll of it. For, there passed not a daie
wherein hee had not that care of his Eele, that it
seemed that hee had not of greater and better matters.
This Eele, being taken about Candelmas, hee meant
to keepe and feede till Lent following, when hee meant
to present him to his Land-lord, for a great gratula-
tion : in the meane-time, hee neuer went out of doores
without giuing warning to his wife and his seruants, to
looke wel to his Eele. When he came in, How doth
mine Eele ? when were you with mine Eele ? who looked
to mine Eele ? I charge you looke well to mine Eele.
Now his wife, a iollie stout Dame, who made more
reckoning of honestie, than either beautie or wisdome
(for she was troubled with neither) had in her house a
young Pie : (which we call a *Magot-a-Pie*). This
Bird, hauing bin hatched in a Neste hard vnder her
chamber window, she chaunced to take into her educa-
tion : and being one that loued to heare a tongue
wagge, either her owne, her Gossips, her Maides, or her
Pyes : for if one were still, the other must be walking :
and when they were all vpon the going, there was no
still-piece of musique : It fell out that this Good-wife,
not a little displeased at her Goose-mans folly in such
so much care ouer the fish, that the flesh was but a
litle set by : one daie, (when her Asseband was gone
forth) sitting with her maid at the wheele, so full at
her heart that yet her tongue would haue swelled if it
had not broke out at her mouth, began thus to fall in
hande with her Maid-seruant : I dare not depose for
her Virginitie, but, as I said, her maid : she fell thus
to breake her minde vnto. Wench, quoth she, doest
thou not see what a sturre thy maister keepes with a
scuruy Eele ? In good earnest a litle thing would make

me take her out of the Cesterne, and put her in a Pye,
or eate her some waie or other : for better haue one
chiding for all then haue such a doe as we haue
about her. In truth, Mistresse, quoth she, (as one
whose mouth hung verie fitting for such a piece of
meate) if it please you, I will quickly ridde you of
this trouble. My maister is ridde to your Landlords,
and there I know he will tarrie to night : if it please
you I will fetch her out of the Cesterne, and kill her,
and flea her, and put her in a Pye, and you may dispatch her ere he come home, or saue a piece for him
when he is quiet after his chiding. Content, wench,
quoth she, I pray thee dispatch her quickly. I warrant
you, quoth shee, forsooth with a trice. Thus was the
Eeles death approaching, and the matter thoroughly
enacted. Now the Pye being made and baked, and
set on the Table, and betwixt the maide and her Dame
(or mistresse) brought to such a passe that there was
very litle left for her master : the *Magot-a-Pye* like a
vyle Bird (that would keepe no counsaile, but duely
would vse her tongue, to talke of all that she saw or
heard) no sooner saw the good-man come into the
house, but (as shee was taught to speake), began with
Welcome home, maister : and then (more then she was
taught), she fell to pratle, Hoh maister, my Dame hath
eaten the Eele : my Dame hath eaten the Eele : my
Dame hath eaten the great Eele. The good man re-
membring his fish, began now to aske his wife, How
doth mine Eele? What meanes the Bird to talke thus
of eating the great Eele? Tush, Husband, quoth she,
warme you I pray you, and goe to bed. It is cold and
late, talke of your Eele tomorrow. No, quoth he, I will
not goe to bed, till I haue seene mine Eele : and

therewith in a bodily feare of that which was fallen out, goes to the Cesterne, and there finding his Eele gonne, comes in againe, as dead at hart as a Stocke-fish, (and yet resolued to brawle out of reason). Comes [Cries?] out : Why hoh ! The good wife, ready to burst with laughing and yet keeping it in with a fayned sigh, sits downe in a chaire, and hangs the head, as though she had had the mother. The maid hauing wit enough, (to make a foole of a tame-goose,) meetes her maister, and catching him in her armes cries out, But softly, maister, be a man, and mooue not all. My dame you know loues you well, and it may be she breedes, and [will] bring you a boye worth twenty bushels of Eeles : saie she had a minde to it, and hath eaten it : if you should seeme to chide for it, it may be a meane to cast her awaie, and that she goes with : and therefore say nothing of it, let it goe. For indeed it is gone. Saist thou so, my Girle ? quoth hee, I thanke thee : hold thee, there is a Tester for thee for thy good counsaile, I warrant thee all shall be well. Then in a goes to his wife, & findes her in her chaire sitting as it were heauily : comes to her and takes her by the hand with, How now wife ? be of good cheere, and take no thought, much good doe thy hart with her, take the rest that are left, if thou haue a minde to them I pray thee. With this, she (as it were awaked out of a trance) said, I thanke you good husband, and so after a few home-complaints, to bed they went, where they agreed so well, that the next morning hee had his part (though it were the least) of that was left, and glad of it too, and so without more adoe goes about his busines. But no sooner was he out of doores, but the mistresse and the maid went to the bird, the *Pye*, and taking her out of the Cage, plucked all the feathers off from her head, and left her as bare as a balde Coote, which in the cold winter was very vncomfortable : which done she was put into the Cage againe, with these wordes, Tell tales againe of the Eele, doe.

Now about dinner time, comes in againe the good-man, and brings in with him a neighbour of his, with a good face, but a balde head, that he had almost no haire on it. Now the Pye being let out of the Cage, no sooner sees this man put off his hat, but she skips on his shoulders and sayes : Oh, your head hath bene puld as well as mine, for telling of tales. You haue told my maister, how my dame eate the great Eele : (and so she would do to any that shee saw bald, that came into the house.) And was not this a merrie iest of the Pye and an Eele?"

Page 46. "Turn I my looks unto the skies."—This poem was doubtless suggested by the following sonnet of Desportes :—

> "Si je me siez à l'ombre, aussi soudainement
> Amour, laissant son arc, s'assied et se repose ;
> Si je pense à des vers, je le voy qui compose ;
> Si je plains mes douleurs, il se plaint hautement.
>   Si je me plains au mal, il accroist mon tourment ;
> Si je respans des pleurs, son visage il arrose ;
> Si je monstre ma playe, en ma poitrine enclose,
> Il defait son bandeau, l'essuyant doucement.
>   Si je vais par les bois, aux bois il m'accompagne ;
> Si je me suis cruel, dans mon sang il se bagne ;
> Si je vais à la guerre, il devient mon soldart.
>   Si je passe la mer, il conduit ma nacelle ;
> Bref, jamais l'importun de moy ne se départ,
> Pour rendre mon désir et ma peine eternelle."

Lodge was fond of this sonnet of Desportes. In

"Scylla's Metamorphosis," 1589, he gives us a literal rendering, which he reprinted (with some alterations) in "Phillis: Honoured with Sundry Poems," 1593. His translation runs thus :—

> " If so I seek the shades I suddenly do see
> The god of love forsake his bow and sit me by ;
> If that I think to write his Muses pliant be,
> If so I plain my grief the wanton boy will cry.
>   If I lament his pride he doth increase my pain ;
> If tears my cheeks attaint, his cheeks are moist with moan ;
> If I disclose the wounds the which my heart hath slain,
> He takes his fascia off and wipes them dry anon.
>   If so I walk the woods, the woods are his delight ;
> If I myself torment, he bathes him in my blood ;
> He will my soldier be if once I went to fight ;
> If seas delight, he steers my bark amid the flood :
>   In brief the cruel God doth never from me go,
>   But makes my lasting love eternal with my woe."

He gives us no inkling that this is a translation.

In making my selections from Lodge, I have confined myself to his romances and to "The Phœnix' Nest." In his "Phillis," we have one of the best of his shorter poems :—

> " Love gilds [1] the roses of thy lips
>   And flies about them like a bee ;
> If I approach he forward skips,
>   And if I kiss he stingeth me.
>
> Love in thine eyes doth build his bower,
>   And sleeps within their pretty shine ;
> And if I look the boy will lower,
>   And from their orbs shoots shafts divine.
>
> Love works thy heart within his fire,
>   And in my tears doth firm the same ;

---

[1] Old ed. " guides,"—evidently a misprint for "guildes."

And if I tempt it will retire,
   And of my plaints doth make a game.

Love, let me cull her choicest flowers ;
   And pity me, and calm her eye ;
Make soft her heart, dissolve her lowers ;
   Then will I praise thy deity.

But if thou do not, Love, I'll truly serve her
In spite of thee, and by firm faith deserve her."

Page 55. "A Song between Wit and Will."—The
Earl of Oxford has a dialogue between Fancy and
Desire which bears some resemblance to this poem of
Breton. It begins :—

" Come hither, shepherd's swain.—Sir, what do you require ?—
I pray thee show to me thy name.—My name is fond Desire. —
When wert thou born, Desire ?—In pomp and prime of May.—
By whom, sweet boy, wert thou begot?—By fond Conceit, men
    say," etc.

See Hannah's " Poems of Sir Walter Raleigh," etc.,
1885, pp. 142-3. Probably both the Earl of Oxford
and Lodge took a hint from a sonnet of Desportes,—

" Amour, quand fus-tu né?—Ce fut lors que la terre
S'émaille de couleurs et les bois de verdeur. —
De qui fus-tu conçeu?—D'une puissante ardeur
Qu' oisiveté lascive en soy-mesmes enserre," etc.

Page 58. " I would thou wert not fair."—This poem
is set to music in John Bartlet's " Book of Airs," 1606.

Page 59. " Friar Bacon."—This popular romance
is of the sixteenth century ; but the earliest extant
edition is dated 1627. Of " George-a-Green " we have
no editions before the eighteenth century.

Page 77. " Beauty sat bathing by a spring."—In
my edition of " England's Helicon " I printed by an

unaccountable oversight, " Beauty sat bathing *in* a spring."

Page 79. " Honour's Academy."—A translation from the French romance of Ollenix du Mont Sacré, *i.e.* Nicolas de Montreux,— " Les Bergeries de Juliette," 1592.

Page 82. " The Spanish Bawd, represented in Celestina," a dramatic romance in twenty-one acts, was translated from the Spanish of Fernando de Rojas. The translator, James Mabbe, assumed the name Don Diego Puede-ser.

Page 85. " The Arcadian Princess " was translated from the Italian of Mariano Silesio, a Florentine, who died in 1368.

Page 86. " Heavenly fair Urania's son."—Samuel Sheppard was a notorious plagiarist. He must have stolen this epithalamium from somebody ; and he certainly seems to have corrupted the text. It would be interesting to discover the genuine original in its integrity. The only other place in which I have met the poem is Joshua Poole's " English Parnassus," 1655, where the text is far more corrupt than in Sheppard's romance.

Page 116. " Choice, Chance, and Change."—This work was published anonymously, but unquestionably it belongs to Nicholas Breton.

Page 138. " The Excuse."—Hannah, in his edition of Raleigh's poems, gives a somewhat different text from Oldys' " Life of Raleigh," p. lv, after " the copy of a celebrated lady, Lady Isabella Thynne, who probably had it out of the family " :—

> " Calling to mind, my *eyes* went long about
> To cause my heart for to forsake my breast,

N

All in a rage I sought to pull them out,
    As who had been such traitors to my rest :
What could they say to win again my grace ?—
Forsooth that they had seen my mistress' face.

Another time, my *heart* I called to mind,—
    Thinking that he this woe on me had brought,
Because that he to love his force resigned,
    When of such wars my fancy never thought :
What could he say when I would him have slain ?—
That he was hers, and had foregone my chain.

At last, when I perceived both eyes and heart
    Excuse themselves, as guiltless of my ill,
I found *myself* the cause of all my smart,
    And told myself that I myself would kill :
Yet when I saw myself to you was true,
I loved myself, because myself loved you."

LIST OF AUTHORS, ETC.

PAGE

FAMOUS HISTORY OF FRIAR BACON 59-61
BRATHWAIT, RICHARD 84-85
BRETON, NICHOLAS 55-58, 89-121

CHETTLE, HENRY 78

DICKENSON, JOHN 53-54

FARLEY, HENRY 83

HISTORY OF GEORGE-A-GREEN 61
GREENE, ROBERT 9-40

LODGE, THOMAS 41-52, 133-137

MABBE, JAMES 82-83
MIRROR OF KNIGHTHOOD 62-74
MUNDAY, ANTHONY 74-78

PHŒNIX' NEST 133-146

RALEIGH, SIR WALTER 138
ROBINSON, CLEMENT (*A Handful of Pleasant
    Delights*) 125-132

SHEPPARD, SAMUEL [?] 86
SIDNEY, SIR PHILIP 1-9

TOFTE, ROBERT 79-80

WROTH, LADY MARY 80-82

YOUNG, BARTHOLOMEW 52